Baiting the Alien
Reeling in the Alien Book 1
Alina Riley

Chapter 1

Iechon

I run my fingers along the handle of my chair as I stare at the map displayed on the window. "So, where are we heading?"

Onner, the kuqnil who is my right ear and who has been helping me a ton, points at the map, though from a distance, it isn't clear which dot he's pointing at. There are many blinking dots that represent different planets. He says, "We're heading to the Milky Way."

I frown. "What are we doing there? That's a boring place to be."

"Mainly, to catch a portal."

I gaze at the map. Between the large window of the spaceship and me, my kuqnils are working on driving the ship and managing its mechanical details. None of them look up unless I specify for them to do so.

I ask Onner, "Are you sure about that? Portals seldom open up there."

All the planets there are dull. Not many beings live on them. The few with intelligent life don't have the technology to interact with the rest of us who can travel between galaxies. There are rules preventing me from contacting them too. All in all, it's a boring place to be.

Onner shrugs as he runs his fingers along the pointy part of his ear. "Well, that's what the forecast said. I think we won't be far off. That's the fastest way we can get back."

I sigh. I suppose... Without a portal, we'll move slower than a dead rock with no hope of getting back there without using up fuel. Calling for someone to tow our spaceship would cost too much.

I stretch my arms. My last client is to blame for this mess. We'd just completed the task of watching out for a group of new traders and making sure they didn't die as they went through a meteorite storm. It was nice money, even though we had to be far away from home, so... I suppose I shouldn't complain.

But we end up in a stupid and boring place because of it.

I ask, "When and where will the portal be?"

"Well, maybe in a day."

I grunt. That's a long time when there isn't anything to do.

Onner chuckles. "Captain, maybe you'll be interested in visiting Earth."

I lift an eyebrow. "What's interesting there?"

"Well, humans live there as the dominant species. They are pretty good with technology, though not as good as us for now."

Yes, and that's how it's going to be boring. I'm not supposed to land there. Not that every being is a rule-follower, but I don't see a reason to be there.

Onner continues, "But they have nice food. At least, that's what I've heard from other traders."

Oh... food... Some species can shift and make themselves look like humans, which makes it easy for them to sneak onto Earth. If I want to try the food, I'll have to conceal myself well or use a device to fool the humans.

I shrug. "I suppose we can go and check it out. It isn't like there are better things to do anyway."

Onner nods. "That's what I thought. We're here anyway. I suppose they'll have something we like. I like human food, but I've never tried human food from Earth."

He isn't wrong. I also like human food, but everything we've tried is from humans that live on other planets. Maybe there will be some difference.

"Get me pizza and a bubble tea," I decide. "I have to check whether they're the same on Earth."

"Can I also get paella?"

Hm... I suppose my crew will like the seafood. "Sure, let's get that too."

It takes a while. I turn around in my seat, tapping my screen to look for interesting things my team can do to earn money. But nothing jumps out at me.

Without a portal and without spending extra fuel on acceleration, the spaceship is so slow.

Onner says to the driving team, "Put up the concealing shield so they won't spot us."

Are we getting close? I stifle a yawn. It's so boring just sitting around. I'm not on shift with something to do, so... staring into the void of the galaxy gets tedious quickly.

We're approaching a blue and green planet with a misty atmosphere. I guess you can't tell if it's an advanced place just from looking at it.

Now we enter the misty part of it. Feels like I'm in a cloud of cotton candy. That's another human food, isn't it? Fluffy, sweet, and sticky all around.

Soon, the white clouds clear out and we arrive close to the seashore. There's sand on the coastline and humans scattered across the sandy ground. Hm...

"Onner, where are we?"

"Earth. I'm searching for restaurants."

I know we're on Earth...

I take a breath to calm myself. Maybe it isn't that important to tell Onner to get smarter when he is searching for food. I suppose I can wait a bit for some nicer food. I tap on my screen to zoom in on the sandy place. I don't like sand; it sticks to me and is rougher than I'd like. Grass is better.

There are human males and females there, some swimming and others running around. I scroll around, but don't see anything chasing after them. Humans have weird leisure activities.

I'm about to stand and take a nap when I scroll to spot a human female in light blue clothes that are in two pieces and only cover her boobs and ass. She has a nice tan and looks like she is ready to tackle the world. There are cartoon lizards on the fabric; maybe they are some type of symbol on Earth.

My heart races. Something about this female is so interesting that my soul is screaming inside me.

I tap and zoom, turning the camera until I can see her face. Her eyes and flowing hair grab me, and my stomach burns with heat.

I have to have this female.

The marking on me burns hot at the thought and my cock twitches. This is different from lust. It's... something more.

"Captain...?"

I blink. Blood is still pooling in my head, smacking the surrounding into silence. I pull my gaze from the screen to Onner's face, which holds concern.

I clear my throat. I want to be angry at him for interrupting my stare at this female. But... the marking on my body burns, and now everything makes sense — she has to be my mate.

"What?"

"I'm asking whether you want paella from this shop."

Onner shows me his phone screen, but I no longer care about food. All I want is my mate.

It doesn't make a lot of sense when she isn't a kuqnil like me, but I know the mating pull, and it's never wrong. Any kuqnil male would know how it feels when it happens.

Maybe I don't understand it now, but soon enough I will. Maybe this human female won't understand either, but she will in time. I will make her understand.

I point at her face on the screen. "I want this one. Get paella and the other food from wherever you want. Just get me this human."

Onner's eyes widen at me. "Are you sure about that? Do you know her?"

I shake my head. Aside from knowing that she is my mate, I know nothing about her. "Not a single clue. But I want her. Get the crew together and get her here for me."

Onner swallows. "Well, Captain, you know that..."

I growl. If Onner won't do it, I'm ready to go do it myself. "I'm the captain and I do what I want. Are you new here? Just tell the guys to be careful, and these humans won't be any wiser. It isn't like I'm getting a dozen or two anyway."

Onner nods. "Okay... I'll arrange that. Make sure nobody sees us and get you this female intact, right?"

Fire surges inside me. "Of course you need to get her to me unscratched. She is going to be my mate and she shall arrive here in pristine condition."

Onner's eyes widen even more, almost as if they are going to fall out of their sockets. "Are you sure about that? A human? Your mate?"

If my screen didn't cost a lot, I would have punched it. If didn't want to have someone to bounce off ideas with, I'd have punched Onner.

"Get me this female!"

"Sure, sure." Onner nods and hurries out of the control room.

I let out a breath, even though fire is still burning inside me. I suppose this trip isn't a waste of time if I find my mate here. But...

I've never talked to a human that's from Earth... And she is a human... But my mating bond doesn't lie... This is going to be confusing.

Chapter 2

Zoe

I sit on my beach towel, staring at the sand ahead. The sun is shining brightly over my head, threatening to roast me alive.

I stretch my arms and lie back on the mat, spread out like a starfish. I close my eyes before the sun can kill me.

It took a long time to save up and plan the vacation, but...

Maybe my expectations were too high. Now... something is missing.

I've been working almost constantly lately. When I get to laze around and do nothing, it feels strange.

What's wrong with me?

I've worked hard and I deserve something nice.

The sound of the waves is calming, something I don't get to enjoy on an ordinary day. I should take my time and relax.

The waves keep coming and the seagulls quack. In the distance, in the sea, people are surfing. I blink. The sun makes me drowsy. Maybe I should take a nap.

I jolt awake when there is a scream. I jump to my feet, only to find kids screaming as they chase the large inflated ball with red and white stripes.

Stupid me. I'm not on duty, so in theory, I don't have to dash off to anyone's rescue.

But I've been a paramedic for so long that it's in my blood. When it looks like something bad is about to happen, I can't stop myself from reacting.

There is a lifeguard here at the beach, and there are others who'll take care of people if get into trouble or hurt themselves. I don't have to worry about that.

I take a sip of my beer out of the can. It was cold when I took it out of the cooler, but now, it isn't as cool. Maybe I should have finished it, or put it back there when I wasn't actively drinking.

The mildly cool drink slides down my throat, sending a chill down my spine. I let out a contented sigh. Soon, I'll be accustomed to the stillness and I can lean into this restful time. Then I'll have all the energy I need to get back to work.

I groan at my own thoughts. Why do I have to keep thinking about work even now, when I'm at the beach?

Maybe I'll meet a handsome man somewhere.

I stare at my bikini with cartoon dinosaurs on it. Maybe I should have worn something that would make me look a bit more mature. But I like this one; it's cute and I don't have many chances to wear it.

Screw whatever people want to think about my taste; if I'm going to meet someone, he should like me for who I am, and maybe also my dinosaur bikini.

I finish the beer and squeeze the can flat before I put it into a plastic garbage bag.

Maybe it is time for another beer.

I reach for the cooler, but there are yells from the direction of the sea.

What's happening there?

Part of me wants to stay and wait it out, but I'm here now; it won't hurt to check things out.

I stand and get off my beach mat. The warm sand seeps into my sandals, even though I try my best to avoid it. There are more people standing there, obscuring my sea view.

How annoying.

My foot sinks into the sand and I feel like a penguin meandering my way to the seaside, shaky and barely managing it. Or maybe penguins would walk better than me. I suppose this is what I signed up for by taking my vacation on a beach.

I take a deep breath and take in the salty scent of the sea. This is a lot better than the smell of disinfectant in the ambulance.

Two lifeguards are in the sea, so maybe someone is drowning. It would be bad if a shark came out of somewhere and snatched them. I laugh at myself. That's something for fiction; definitely not a good thing to ever happen in real life. This beach has never had a single sighting of sharks anyway, so that won't ever happen.

The lifeguards reach out with the floating ring. It doesn't take long before the three are back on the beach.

The one who was drowning is a teenage boy; maybe he fell from his surfboard at just the wrong time and got choked by water. The lifeguards bring him onto the beach and start helping him.

So... nothing much to watch anymore. The crowd seems to catch on too and people start going back to their own spots.

I stare at the sea. Should I give swimming a try? I would get wet though. Maybe I shouldn't swim after I've drunk a beer and plan to drink another.

I turn back to my spot, only to see my cooler gone. Well, some fool is running away with it!

I pick up speed and dash toward that man. Who the hell would wear long sleeves and gloves on a hot summer day? He even has long trousers that, combined with his clothes, cover his whole body.

"Hey, you! I see you! Put my stuff down!"

He or she, whatever they are, picks up speed. I just want my beer back. Who even puts valuables in a cooler anyway?

That person runs all the way to the small store in the middle of the beach. That stupid store is somehow closed, which sent me off my plan and I ended up having to buy my beer somewhere else - again.

But this fool still doesn't get to take my stuff.

I struggle while swearing at the sand for slowing me down; if this was a normal road, I'd be a lot faster.

That person takes a turn behind the store as if I won't catch him. Does he think I'm that dumb?

I turn the corner, halting when there is a shadow ahead. I jump, but something smacks me on the head.

The pain spreads through me with a spark spiking through me; my limbs grow numb and I can't move my body anymore.

Darkness grabs me and forces itself through my vision.

"Did you get the right one?"

"I think so?"

"Captain said... what kind of clothes again?"

"Cartoon Earth lizards."

"Oh, then we probably have the right one."

"Let's go before someone catches us."

"It's so damn hot here."

What the hell is happening? Who are these people?

A stronger spark rushes through me and I can no longer feel anything, not even my own existence.

Chapter 3

Zoe

"I've told you to be careful when you get her for me!"

The voice is a masculine growl. My head throbs and my body feels numb, and I can't remember what happened.

Where am I?

Who is that?

Who is he talking to?

He can't be talking to me, right?

Argh...

My head hurts. I shiver in the cold. My eyes are still closed and my eyelids are too heavy to lift.

"Sorry, Captain. We tried our best. We didn't do much anyway, but we had to be careful so she wouldn't keep struggling. We weren't supposed to let anyone see us." This is another male, his voice quivering.

Who is this captain? He must be the one who plotted to kidnap me. He has to be.

I hate him already. What could I have done to wrong anyone?

"Captain, I think she moved." This is yet another male. Something's seriously wrong here!

"If this is your plan to divert my attention—! Wait... Get out of here."

Yes, I know; I'm the one moving and fighting to open my eyes.

Did I get captured by human traffickers?

But in the middle of a beach in the summer season, with dozens of people around?

There must have been easier targets, not that I wish that fate on anyone.

There is a hiss followed by a click of something, probably the door.

"Female, wake up. I know you're awake."

My head aches like hell because of this man, yet he blames me as if it is my fault that I'm not fully awake?

I have to fight to open my eyes. There is a weak spark of electricity flowing through me. There are tingles at my fingertips as if I have folded them for too long, only releasing them just now.

It must be the taser thing those men used to kidnap me.

My vision remains blurry for another moment before it focuses.

In front of me, there is a green man with pointy ears; his nose is pointier than most people I've ever met. His eyes are intense on me — an intensity that's more beastly than human-like.

Who is this? He's green and half-naked with tattoos all over his body.

I groan. "What the fuck? You're a bit too early for Halloween, dumbass."

He growls and comes closer to the bed I'm sitting on.

He is huge, a lot larger than he looks from a distance away. He's probably eight feet tall and packed to the brim with muscles.

I swallow. I did hope to run into a handsome man during my holiday, but this isn't what I meant!

Heat pools in me even though it's stupid given the situation I'm in. This man has a vibe that screams how I should be more afraid of him than I currently am.

But this man is also the reason I'm here, in an unknown place, surrounded by stupidity.

I scowl. "What's the growl for? You fucking moron. This is so dumb."

"You called me a... dumbass? This is human's way of insulting, right?"

What the actual fuck is that? A human's way of insulting? Does he think I'm that dumb?

"You! What's wrong with you? Painting yourself green is so pathetic. I don't know you. Let me go."

He laughs. "Of course, I never expected you to know me. More importantly, you are here now and you're mine."

Huh?

I suppose he isn't here to kill me, but there can be a lot of things that are worse than being dead.

"Dude, you're crazy. I don't belong to anyone. Where am I?"

"On my spaceship."

I burst out laughing. "Seriously? Your spaceship? Is that what you call your mother's basement?"

He growls and yanks my hair, lifting me off the bed. "Maybe you should stop insulting me. Otherwise, you will regret it."

"What?" I reach for his pointy ear. "You're the one messing with me. If you think it's funny to prank me by dressing up—" I yank the ear and he hisses. The pointy part seems to be glued tightly onto his skull. "You've put on an elaborate costume."

"Stop pulling my ear! I'm not a human!"

He isn't... a human?

I grunt when he drops me onto the bed again. I gasp when I check my fingers.

None of the green has flaked off. It looks like he has nice paint on his body too.

I roll my eyes. "It's okay, you've pranked me. I'm so scared now. Take off the silly pointy ears."

"I don't know what you are talking about. Those are my ears and I can't take them off. I don't think humans can take their ears off either."

"Humans this and humans that. What's wrong with you? Thinking that you're cute by pretending to be an alien?"

He rolls his eyes. "Alien is what humans call us, I suppose. I'm not pretending to be an alien; I am an alien. I know you may not understand, but it is what it is. I'm not a human."

I swallow and stare at him. Part of me wants to laugh at how silly he and this whole situation is.

But... his glare makes him look a lot more serious, so I don't dare to keep laughing.

"So... if you said I'm on a spaceship, show me some evidence."

He lifts an eyebrow. "You don't believe me? I'm going to let that slide just this once; you will learn."

He goes to the grey wall of this stupid room and presses a button.

The grey wall warps and shows a dark space. There are many shiny spots out there that aren't moving.

I roll my eyes. "A projector and a picture of space? I've seen that. Do I look that dumb — dumb enough you think you can fool me with that?"

He squints at me. "If you weren't my mate, I would have already made you regret your words."

I'm what? His mate? What the hell is wrong with him? He seems crazier than me.

He hisses. "Actually, you should be able to figure that out just by looking at me. I don't look like a human at all."

I blink and eye him up and down. I suppose he isn't wrong, but...

"Bro, you are just too early for Halloween."

"I have no idea what 'Halloween' means. Is that one of your Earth months?"

I stare at my fingers, which I grabbed his ear with. Even if that's amazing body paint, some should have rubbed off onto my finger.

"You can't be an alien. Where am I, other than on your spaceship?"

He clicks his tongue. "Well, we caught a portal to get far away from Earth before someone saw my ship. We're a few galaxies away now, getting close to a space station."

My heart skips a beat. Either he's crazy, or I'm crazy.

I shake my head. "No way, that's impossible. You can't be an alien, and you're just messing with me. I don't know what you want with me by kidnapping me off a busy beach. But please... stop messing with me."

"Maybe you don't understand at this moment, but you will soon. I don't mean to hurt you, but I don't have another choice. You can pretend as if I'm fooling you for now, but there's no changing the fact that you're on my ship now."

I suck in a breath. My head hurts when I try to piece things together. Am I an idiot for believing him for even a single moment?

If I'm a few galaxies away from Earth, then my vacation as I planned is definitely over.

Even if he's just a crazy human with the delusion of being an alien who has locked me up somewhere on Earth, I still have to convince him to let me go. And while I'm at it, maybe I can have some fun.

I shrug and lean back against the headboard of the bed. "Well, I was taking a vacation on a sunny beach with a nice sea; but now here you've made me stay for some reason. Now I'm bored and I suppose you have to keep me entertained now?"

His eyes darkened. "Oh, keep you entertained? I already have an idea that will make you scream and moan."

My heart skips a beat; the heat inside of me starts to grow again.

He's huge – how would it feel if he pins me down and takes me roughly?

I blink at how crazy my thoughts are. But maybe that will help me to figure out whether he's just pretending to be an alien.

If he really is an alien, I suppose he has something interesting and very different from humans hiding under his trousers.

Chapter 4

Zoe

I stare at this green male as he grabs my hair again. I swallow when I can't pull my eyes away from his trousers. He's wearing something that looks shiny, but not like the fabric of my sports shorts. It is... something else.

And... maybe I shouldn't, but I keep staring at the bulge between his legs. It looks like he is hiding a cobra there and he is going to fuck me so hard that I won't be able to walk again.

"My mate, I have what is needed to keep you entertained a lot better than the sandy place on that strange and backward planet."

I shiver from the intensity of his voice. He's still delusional to be saying that I'm his mate or something. I don't even understand what that means.

But...

He takes my hand and puts it on his cock. I stare at him, and can't even believe how huge he is.

He grins and his cock twitches. "Like what you feel? I can make sure you are very happy and I can please you better than any human male."

I suck in a breath. After I kept teasing him, it won't make any sense for me to act like I want him. I'm not going to give him the satisfaction.

I shrug and take my hand off his cock. "Well, is that what you think? I hope I won't get bored. Maybe you aren't even better than a human male."

He growls, and he pins me on the bed with his strong hands on my shoulders.

I shiver as I stare at him. He looks a lot stronger and larger when he hovers over me with fire in his eyes.

My pussy clenches and I swear I'm getting wet just from this. What's wrong with me?

He narrows his eyes on me. "Or, maybe you like to be taken hard. Is that the case?"

My heart skips a beat, and I fight to hide my emotion. "No, I'm just wondering what you can do. I have standards. Just a cock probably won't clear them."

"You will soon regret that. Just admit it – you want me."

The surge of heat grows stronger inside me. It's so tempting to be enjoying him already. I'm not sure what he can give me, but that will probably be better than us staring at each other.

If he plans on selling me to some scary space pirates or space kidnappers, I may as well enjoy the time when I'm still alive.

I roll my eyes. "I suppose I'm giving you a chance when you kidnapped me and I can't even enjoy my vacation."

He growls and whips out his cock.

Fuck!

His cock is huge and matches his large body. Maybe I should have anticipated that, but he is larger than I expected. His cock is green like him, also with tattoos.

I don't think a sane human would tattoo his cock, so...

Maybe he is an alien. That would make a lot more sense.

He strokes his cock as if showing off his size and making sure I have enough time to stare at it. "Wait for it. I like it when you act like a brat. What people on Earth refer to as playing hard to get."

I can only try my best not to burst out in laughter. He says the most hilarious things with the most serious face I've seen in a while.

He grabs my bikini and yanks it off me. I moan and squirm. "If you dare to break my favorite bikini, you are screwed."

He halts when the bikini is coming off my ass, almost revealing my pussy. "What? You mean I can't break this? I was looking forward to tearing it off you."

Is that even a question? "No, you don't get to do that."

"Well..." He swallows audibly. "I suppose..."

He slows down and takes my bikini off me as if he is being careful and making sure he will keep that piece of fabric intact.

I have no idea what's wrong with him.

He tosses my bikini to the side. I suppose it makes it easy for him to strip me naked, compared to when I would be in a t-shirt and trousers instead.

He grabs my boobs and rubs his tip against my wet pussy.

"This is soaking wet. What does it mean?"

I gasp. His cock is cold. This is very different from anything I could have expected. And his question annoys me.

If he looked exactly like a man, I would have growled and refused to talk to him, but... The way he asked. Maybe it is a genuine question, and he isn't trying to dirty talk his way with me.

He moves to sniff between my legs. The tip of his nose pokes at my pussy. "Are you not feeling well?"

"You are boring as fuck. For someone who claims to be my mate, you know oddly little about me and my species."

I give up. For my pleasure, maybe I will play along and pretend he actually is an alien.

He looks up from my pussy and grins. "Maybe this means you are ready for me."

He rubs his cock at my entrance again.

I stare at his cock as he pushes into me. He is so fucking huge that he stretches me.

And—

Fuck!

He is deceivingly huge with something hard along his cock, something like ridges that feels like the spikes on the back of dinosaurs.

His cock is so cold that as he pushes into me, my body burns hotter to get used to his coldness.

I've never imagined this, but his cold cock is even better than a hot human cock.

He shudders when my pussy squeezes him. "You are so tight. I know human females are tight down there, but this is better than I imagined."

"Looks like you are the one enjoying what you get. Happy to get my kidnapped pussy? I suppose you can bore me to death now."

He grunts and rests his hand on my throat. "I like you this way."

This is some crazy talk. I'm about to yell at him when he shoves all the way into the deepest of me and starts driving in and out of me. The ridges on his cock rub my wall so hard that pleasure explodes in me and my body moves with his strokes.

He grunts as he picks up speed. "You are so amazing, so perfect for me."

He is huge and when I wrap my arms around him, I can't hold him completely. He has me pinned on the bed while slamming his cock into me, devouring me the way he wants.

I grit my teeth, fighting my moans. I hate how amazing he feels and I don't want to stroke his ego.

His ass still kidnapped me and I shouldn't enjoy this, not like this.

He pecks a kiss on my forehead, picking up speed. "Don't be ashamed. You can enjoy me."

I hate him. My body tenses when he shoves his hard and thick rod in and out of me. The pleasure is so strong that it cracks me and I scream as my body tenses.

"Fuck!" I close my eyes when it gets a bit too much. "You are such a fucking maniac."

He growls, "I don't think that's praise. I'd be smarter if I were you."

I squeeze his shoulder as I moan again and again. His thick cock rams orgasm followed by orgasm through me.

"I'm going to fill you up."

I gasp when he holds my throat. He knows what he's doing, even though it makes no sense at all.

My legs wrap tighter around him before I can give that any thought.

His cock twitches inside me and he shoves himself into the deepest part of me. "You are so amazing, my mate."

I gasp when his hot cum fills me. His cum is so hot that he burns another orgasm through me.

This is still a fucking crazy creature. But he seems to know my body well and maybe I shouldn't complain too much.

He grins when he pulls out of me. "You look so sexy with my cum dripping out of your hole."

I shiver when the heat grows in me again, echoing through my body from my pussy. There is a pull inside me, seemingly pulling my heart to him.

This is strange. But I suppose it isn't too bad.

He sits on the bed by my side with a grin. His cock is still fully erect, looking like he can keep fucking me for a lot longer.

If this is how my vacation will be, mght not be that bad.

He asks, "Are you feeling it?"

The orgasm and the pleasure. "Yes." I can barely manage to squeeze the words out of me.

He nods. "I told you. You are going to love this."

I still think he is crazy, but maybe crazy in a not-that-bad way.

He rests his hand on my stomach. "I can almost feel my cum inside you."

The way he says it seems to mean something more, but...

My brain is foggy. Everything happened a bit too fast for my mind to comprehend. "I suppose?"

He grins. "Good. Now, you will wait for me here while I talk to my warriors."

What warriors? Those people that pretended to be aliens with him?

I roll my eyes. But if this means he will leave me alone for now, that's not too bad. "You've found a bunch of delusional people to go along with you."

He hisses and his cock twitches. "Who is delusional? Stop your stupidity."

I shrug when he puts on his trousers. "You got a good costume."

"I thought you were smart enough to have figured that out. I'm not a human. Which part of me looks human?" He spreads his arms with a deep scowl, which makes him pretty handsome.

Most of his features don't look human... and I don't know who would plan such a scheme just to kidnap me, but... I don't feel like letting him have an easy time and it seems like he hates it when I call him a human. Maybe I will keep that up for another while.

"You have arms and legs."

He stares at his arms. "Really? This is the dumbest thing I've ever heard!"

"Oh, and you somehow speak my language. I thought aliens should have something special for themselves. What are the odds?"

I'm so smart.

He scowls and says something that I don't understand.

I shrug. "You're trying too hard. You're just making random noises. Want to pass that off as another language?"

He hisses. "Stop it. I only speak in your language because I want you to understand me."

Haha. "No, I don't believe you. Why do you know my language if you swear you aren't a human?"

He folds his arms. "Well, there are humans on other planets, too. I do trade with them, so I know a few human languages. What's the problem? I also know the language of nogzuls, nekrozzros, and baekexes."

I have no idea what those words mean. Maybe that's other species of aliens, or maybe he's making things up.

He sighs. "I don't know my mate is such a stubborn female. Maybe you need some time to think about it."

"What's your species called?"

"I'm a kuqnil."

He doesn't spend a single second thinking, so either he is completely making it up or he is speaking the truth.

I ask, "Your name?"

"Iechon. But others call me the captain here."

Well, that's not a human name. Or he's still making things up. "Do you know my name?"

He shakes his head. "Not a single clue."

I squint at him. "Really?"

"You are the one with the cute clothes. And my mate. I'm not going to pass you up when I see you. You may have doubts, but you will soon understand."

Here he goes again, such a crazy man.

"You still don't even know my name. It looks like you don't plan to find out. For you, a mate is just a female body for you to fuck?" I shiver at my own words. It feels

like I'm calling myself a fucktoy or something, which...
strangely lights a fire inside me.

His eyes narrow. "I believe you will tell me your name
very soon, maybe now."

He has such an ego.

"I'm Zoe."

"That's a nice name. Zoe."

"Yes, Zoe."

He opens his mouth, but there is a mechanical beep.
He scowls and picks up his phone from the bedside
table. He checks it and glances at me. "You are to stay
here and wait for me. If I catch you wandering somewhere you shouldn't, you will regret it."

I suck in a breath at his intense glare. I suppose
whether he is an alien or not, I should listen. Or... maybe
this will be my chance to flee.

Chapter 5

Iechon

After I put on my trousers and my cape, I leave my room, but not without giving my mate a glare to make sure she knows to listen to me.

I hate to leave the room when my mate still doesn't seem convinced that I'm not a human.

I don't understand. Is that because she is a human? Are all humans like that?

My cock twitches as I walk down the corridor to the control center. If only I could keep her pinned under me for longer.

Human females feel so good. I wonder whether she is special.

I feel the tip of my ear. I'm definitely not a human, but she mentioned something called Hallow... I don't remember, maybe I should look it up. Humans probably have interesting culture on Earth.

More importantly, I love her in her cute clothes. She must know I'm going to be around and thus wears clothes that barely cover her boobs and that pussy.

I'll ignore how there were other females that wear similar clothes as her on the sandy ground. She is mine.

I take a deep breath when the marking on me burns hot. This has to be how the mate bond feels. I've heard about that, but I could only imagine before. Now, I feel it in my body. It is something more than lust, something I have never felt before.

I press the button for the door to open. After the faint hissing noise, I go into the control center. All the Kuqnils stand and bow their heads at me. I nod for them to be seated and get back to their work.

Onner bows his head at me as I take my seat in the center of the control room.

I ask, "What did you call me for?"

"Captain, we are ready for another portal jump. Where should we go?"

I rub my ear. I haven't planned that far ahead. We were distracted when I sensed my mate. Now, we should probably get back to the trading route. "Do we have another trade ready for us?"

"Well, we have prospects. There is a group of zalcors looking to go somewhere within the Empire."

I lift an eyebrow. "As a rule, we don't try to anger the Empire's minions."

The Empire gives us business too, not that I love to take their money. I like money, but I would rather take it from better sources. I only do what doesn't feel like selling my soul.

Onner lets out a soft sigh. "I know, but they pay handsomely."

"But they're zalcors."

Zalcors are the ones that show up and disappear whenever they want to. They are strong and they fight the Empire, which I respect. But when it comes to having close contact with them...

Onner sighs. "The risk is a bit too high, I suppose."

"Why do they want help? I would think they could do it themselves and keep their trail hidden."

If the zalcors are looking for someone else to take the heat, I'm not interested. I continue, "We transport things for beings, not die for them."

Onner shrugs. "We won't have to get into the Empire's territory. They said they want cargo delivered to a planet within the Alliance and it shouldn't make us suspicious."

I shake my head. "No, I'm not interested. We aren't that short of cash."

Onner nods. "I suppose. But we still need a destination."

Except I don't want to care about that at this moment. All I want is to enjoy my mate.

"Let's get to the space station and we can celebrate."

"Celebrate what?"

I don't think we need those details. "Something. Just figure it out. I'm busy."

"But captain!" Onner follows me through the door despite my long stride, clearly having no intention of staying.

When the door closes behind me, Onner is still there. I turn around. "What's the issue?"

He halts and shakes his head. "Nothing much. Just... want to check in about the human you got."

I scowl. "What's wrong?"

"What are you going to do with her?"

"She's mine now."

"So... she triggered the mate bond?"

"I think so." I suck in a breath while I say the words. If we aren't in the corridor on our own with no one around, I wouldn't have said that. Somehow, it feels weird to let someone else know my private business.

"She's a human."

"Yes, but I feel it in my blood. Are you here to argue with me?" I hiss and flex my body. If Onner wants to fight me for her, he can try, but he won't get her.

There is a fire inside me, and that's something I've never felt before either. It is different from how Zoe makes me feel. This fire is a lot stronger and it burns my stomach so hard that I want to punch Onner.

Onner shakes his head. "Not at all, Captain. Has she accepted the mate bond?"

Yes?

I have no idea. She seems to like how I fucked her and she came for me, but...

Onner lifts his brows. Now his snobbish face is laughing at me and I should—

"Captain, I hope you aren't trying to make her do things."

I groan. "No, I didn't. Why would I do that?"

"It looks like she hasn't agreed to the bond."

"How did you know?" I resist the urge to punch him, even though he's asking for it. I hadn't told him. There should be no reason he knows about that.

"You hesitated. I've talked to those who have found their mate. They are certain about the bond."

I suppose... I feel the bond, but I'm not sure whether it is completed. When I fucked her, the heat was the same as when I first saw her on the screen. Maybe I haven't completed the bond.

He says, "Captain, be careful. You can't force her."

I roll my eyes. "She will understand soon enough. I will make her my mate and I will prove you wrong. She will know I'm her mate."

I take a breath and put my finger back to my side. I didn't realize I was pointing at the ceiling for no reason.

"That's not how that works."

I grunt and turn away to the corridor, going down the path to my own. "Get back there."

He nods and goes back to the control room while I go and look for my mate.

Where is Zoe? I miss her already. My cute little brat. I smirk as my cock twitches. If she still doesn't understand, she will, very soon.

Chapter 6

Zoe

I peek at the door, resting my ear on it. Is that strange guy gone now?

He said I should stay in the room, but what if I don't want to?

Maybe I just have to open the door and I'll be free again. Maybe he's been fooling me and thinking that I'm dumb enough to buy into his lies.

My heart throbs in my chest and his cum in me screams otherwise.

I shake my head. I'm fooling myself. Maybe he can make me feel great and his interesting cock with ridges made me come like never before, that doesn't mean he can kidnap me and lock me up in a room and claim to be an alien.

I put my finger on the silvery button he pressed for the door to open. I shiver when my fingertip lands on the cool metal surface of the button.

He said I would regret it if I left. But maybe I'll regret it more if I don't give it a try. Maybe he's fun to stay with and fuck, but I have my own life to live.

And my beer.

Maybe I won't get my cooler and my beer back, but I may still get part of my vacation on the beach, listening to the sea instead of a guy who keeps insisting I'm his mate.

I press the button and the door slides open. The corridor outside is quiet. There is a low humming noise, probably from some kind of engine.

I could be on a ship, or a spaceship.

I laugh at myself. Probably a ship. That would make more sense, since I was kidnapped on the beach.

Maybe I should believe the guy when he insists that he is an alien. But... That sounds so silly that I can't take him seriously without making my head hurt.

I peek at the two sides of the corridor. Cold air is moving, there is ventilation here, and...

I shiver when I remember that I'm naked. I go back to the bed to find my bikini tossed to the side. At least I warned that crazy man not to destroy it.

I put them on, though the bikini won't hide too much of me away from the others' gazes.

The corridor is cold. Maybe the green costume makes him hot and therefore he turns the fans all the way up. Such a pretentious guy. Some people are a bit too fond of aliens; maybe that makes them feel special or amazing.

Better than me.

I scowl. That's annoying and I hate people like that.

I put my foot outside. There isn't a single alarm. I suppose I should get going and figure out where I am.

It can't be that hard.

There is still no one in the corridor. There isn't a noise from either end. There isn't a sign on the wall, so I suppose I'm going to have to pick a side.

Right, that way.

As a paramedic, sometimes I rely on my instinct to figure out what happened to those people who called us to a scene. It would be a lot more efficient if they can tell me what happened. But sometimes, everyone is frantic and too frightened to even make out the words.

I go down the corridor, shivering as the wind blows over me. Whoever lives here is crazy.

My bikini is perfect for my beach vacation, but when it's freezing cold here...

"Hey! What are you doing here?"

Fuck!

I set off running without looking behind me to see who that is. It is a man, not the crazy one that I fucked, but... someone working for that guy can't be good either.

I storm my way down the corridor, turning the corners and trying my best to get going. There are doors to the sides with buttons, but those look like other bedrooms. There are a fuck ton of crazy men here. Maybe all of them think that they're aliens. Why not unicorns?

I turn another corner. There is a large figure in front of me. I hurry to halt, but I've been running too quickly to stop in time.

"Grrr...."

Fuck! I know the noise...

It's the green guy. Iechon, if I remember his name correctly.

I force a smile when he grabs my throat with his huge hand. I pat his hand with mine. "Hey... Nice to see you here."

He hisses. "I thought I warned you."

I swallow. He did. Maybe I should have listened.

There are messy footsteps behind me, coming at me. Whoever it is says, "Captain."

Iechon looks up and nods. "It's okay. I have her now."

"Sure, I will head back to my position."

Iechon nods and there are footsteps again, walking past us. That is another green guy with similarly pointy ears. I can't see his face, but maybe he also has a pointy nose. He is shorter and not as muscular as Iechon, but he is also huge.

What's the odds of more than one guy that's taller than seven feet?

"I said, look at me."

I blink and pull my gaze from that guy's back to Iechon. "Yes?"

He runs his finger along my face with his other hand still on my neck. "I said I warned you not to step out of my room."

Fuck him... I'm not his property and he doesn't get to tell me what to do.

I swallow. "You did."

"Yes, then, why are you here? Running down the corridor? Are you trying to flee?" His growl echoes in the corridor and my legs grow weak as if I will crumble into pieces in no time. He is a huge man, so when he towers over me and glares at me...

Maybe I'm too small to fight him and maybe I have to try my best, otherwise, I really will regret it.

I rub his stomach when he has yanked me off the floor and I can't reach his cock. "I was trying to look for you."

His eyes narrow on me, and don't seem convinced. I wouldn't be convinced just by that, either. I suppose I have to give a better reason than that.

"Iechon," I put up my best cute face. "How could you leave me alone in that room? It's cold there and I can't snuggle with you. You said I'm your mate."

He muses and lets go of me. I'm not expecting that and I stumble when my feet have to stand on their own with short notice.

"Oh!" He grabs me and pulls me into his arms, as if he hasn't expected me to fall. He was the one letting go of me without a single warning and now, it seems like he thinks that I'm the problem.

He rubs my side with his muscular arms that somehow light an annoying flame in my stomach. Why is my body reacting to his touch? He is the delusional one who kidnapped me.

He pecks a kiss on my cheek, holding me so tightly that I would never be able to flee. "I'm really sorry. I don't mean to leave you alone. Are you cold?"

That's the stupidest question I've ever heard. I'm in my bikini and he has the air-conditioning on as if it doesn't cost him money to do that.

"You make me warm."

He hums with a proud smile. I think he won't remember to punish me by now. He squeezes my ass. "You are not wrong. But you're my mate, so you shouldn't be here for everyone to look at."

Please don't tell me he's trying to lock me up again.

Now that he isn't grabbing my throat, I can reach for his cock, but that means he'll put me on his bed again, so...

I stroke his chest. "Will you show me your spaceship? I've never been on one."

He watches me. If this is an actual spaceship, I don't think I can go anywhere. Maybe I don't know a lot about spaceships, but I know enough to know that I will die if I open the door and jump outside.

He nods. "Sure, I'll show you around. You are my mate, so you get to see everything."

Phew...

He turns to the side of the corridor where he came from. "You are going to love this place."

I don't. This is a stupid, cold place. I don't understand how he can still be mostly half-naked. He's wearing a cape and trousers, and that's all.

He nudges my side, rubbing me as if he is trying to keep me warm. I silently sigh. It seems like he's crazy about me, and I'm not sure whether that's a good thing.

He shouts something down the corridor. I don't understand the words, but someone answers, also talking in that foreign-sounding language.

Maybe when he said that he was an alien, he wasn't lying. Otherwise, he would have to invent a whole language and make everyone here play along. That seems to be a bit too much effort for human traffickers.

We head toward the huge door at the end of the corridor. Maybe that's an important place. By my side, there is a low hiss and the door opens. From inside comes another green man with a cape in his hand. He says something to Iechon, and Iechon takes the cape from him, putting it around my shoulders.

"Is this better?"

It's a leather cape. I run my fingers along it. It is smooth but lighter than it seems. So... probably not leather, just similar to leather. It's a long cape for me. It covers his ass, but for me, it feels like a dress that goes down all the way to my ankles.

He tilts his head to the side as he watches me. "Looks like you are a bit too short for this."

"Or this is too long for me." I spread my hands at my sides, letting the cape hang on me. "But thank you. It helps."

He hums and nods. "I think I will get new clothes that fit you soon. Sadly, all I have here on the ship are clothes like these." He gestures at his cape and his trousers. "But we will get to the space station and you will get anything that you can imagine. Given you come from Earth, I suppose you will also be getting things you can't even imagine."

Well... I don't think getting back to Earth and spending my vacation as I planned is on his list.

He pulls me to his side again. "Now, let's keep going and I shall show you around."

Yeah... I'm so excited to see what he has...

Chapter 7

Zoe

The door in front of us slides open, revealing a dozen green beings like Iechon sitting in a half-circle, all of them facing the window. There are the low humming noises of engines and the occasional beeps of machines. There are also tapping noises. Maybe some of these green men are typing something or pressing buttons.

They stand when we show up, and they turn to us.

I freeze at my spot. All of them are green like Iechon, but they have different facial features; clearly the same species. I suppose assuming they're costumes is going to make me look dumb by now.

Iechon nods and gestures at me. "This is Zoe, and you will respect her like you respect me."

All the eyes are on me briefly before they drop their gazes. Maybe this is their way of respecting me.

Iechon continues, "Now, get back to work. We'll have a celebration soon."

What celebration? I hope that has nothing to do with kidnapping me or selling me. If Iechon plans to sell me off, I suppose there's no need to tell his crew to respect me.

So... he really thinks I'm his mate or something like that, which I still don't fully understand?

Iechon nudges my side and gestures at the dashboard. I follow him and walk down the stairs to the working beings. He points at the window. "As you can see, we are making progress and getting to a portal. Onner!"

A green man stumbles his way down the stairs to our side. He wasn't at the dashboard working with the others, so maybe he is a bit more important than the rest.

"Captain, we are searching for a portal as you instructed. We will be arriving in a few hours."

Iechon nods with a smile. "Good. We will find clothes with cute lizards for Zoe."

Cute lizards? The cartoon dinosaurs on my bikini? Fuck...

Now that I remember that I'm still wearing those... I silently sigh. I do like the cartoon dinosaurs, but... maybe Iechon is misunderstanding something, and I have no idea how I can change his mind.

Not that I'm ashamed of wearing these, but... it's silly to think that cartoon dinosaurs are essential to my life.

Onner nods. "I'm sure we can find something for humans there."

Iechon says, "Good, keep me updated."

Onner leaves and heads back to the stairs. I stare at him until he goes back to the side of a larger chair with its own floating table. He stands without sitting. Maybe that seat is meant for Iechon.

Iechon points at the window. "Look at all the planets out there. It is impressive, right?"

I pull my gaze from Onner to the window. Outside, there are a lot of shiny dots, which should be the planets. It is almost as if I am staring at the photo of the galaxy, except it's a lot clearer, and...

I almost forgot to breathe, until my lungs hurt to remind me. This can't be a video. It feels real, and I can feel it inside me. "Iechon..."

"Yes?"

"So... you really aren't human."

He scowls. "I thought we dealt with that already and you understand that."

"You're an alien..." My heart skips a beat and blood drains from my head.

He scoffs. "I suppose that's what some humans call us. Yes, aliens, if that helps with your understanding."

I blink. My brain is still empty. "So... I was kidnapped by an alien."

He rolls his eyes. "I don't see it that way. You are my mate and you are meant to stay with me. I'm glad I found you, so here you are."

Yeah... That sounds like exactly how kidnapping works.

"You sent someone to knock me out on the beach and yanked me away from my vacation without even asking whether I want to be here or not."

His eyes narrow on me. "What do you mean? Why would you not want to be here with me? Why would you want to be on a backward planet like Earth? There's nothing interesting there."

I suck in a breath as fury brews inside me. This is absolutely disrespectful. I'm not something he can decide to take whenever and wherever he wants, and maybe Earth isn't as advanced as they are, but calling it backward is rude.

"Stop saying it like that. Earth is where I grew up and where I belong."

He scowls. "No, you are staying here with me and you are going to be my mate."

I push him to the side, but he is too heavy and too large for me to move him more than an inch. I take a step away from him instead. "No, I'm going back. Let me go."

He growls, "No. I said you are here to stay and you are mine."

I shiver when he takes a step closer to me. He is a hulky alien and he could crush me if he wanted to. But... I'm not going to apologize. He should be ashamed of himself. I open my mouth when he hisses at me again.

Words linger on the tip of my tongue. I'm not going to let this alien walk all over me. I...

His glare seems to burn holes in me and all my instincts shout at me to shut up. But I've never been good at that.

Yet...

There is a beep on the dashboard. My gaze darts to the machine and I remember there are other green males around. Maybe that's part of the reason Iechon is mad.

Geez... he has quite an ego. He refuses to look weak in front of these aliens who work for him?

I sigh. "We'll talk about that."

Iechon nods, even though the beep is gone by now. "You will understand very soon. Are you hungry?"

"Yes."

That's what I said, but I'm not exactly hungry. The storm in my stomach is still raging and my fists are still clenched even though I don't remember clenching them in the first place. Food will be a good excuse for us to get out of this room.

Iechon reaches for my hand and I let him take it. I have to ask him about this mate thing. No doubt he is going to keep me here, but at least I have to understand what he is looking for, other than my physical presence.

Chapter 8

Iechon

I sit at the table in one of the meeting rooms, watching Zoe eat.

We bought a bit too much food from Earth before we left, so I give her some of the paella. She is taking her time eating. I think she is just trying to delay our talk.

She should know that this is my spaceship and what I say goes, and that also includes her. She should listen to me and she shouldn't even imagine arguing with me in front of others.

She may be my mate, but that doesn't mean she gets to disrespect me.

I clear my throat. "Are you done with the food?"

She puts down the spoon and scowls at me. "Can't you see? I'm not done yet."

I growl. There are only the two of us here, and I'm not going to let her loose again. She has disrespected me more times than I could count since she woke up.

She shivers and tenses. My heart almost stops. Did I... do something wrong?

I don't think I did, but growling at her doesn't feel right. My gut is screaming at me to treat her better. But I don't understand what's not right.

I clear my throat. "You said you want to talk to me. What's that about?"

She picks up the spoon again and pushes the few grains of rice on the plate. How dare she avoid answering my question and pretend to not hear me?

I'm about to growl at her and demand my answer when there is a sniffing noise from her. It is faint as if she is trying to hold it in. I can only see the top of her head, so I reach for her cheek.

She ducks away from my finger as if there's something wrong with me. How dare she? Does she think that she gets to do whatever she wants just because she is my mate?

Enough is enough, and I—

"Iechon..."

I grit my teeth and push the fire down into my stomach, forcing a more gentle voice. "What?"

"I don't like it when you shout at me."

What the actual—!

The sniffing noise is there again, and pain surges inside me. Something is wrong, even though I don't know what that is. I ask, "What's wrong?"

"Huh?" She finally looks me in the eye. There is a ring of red around her eyes and it hurts me seeing that. "Are you asking what's wrong with you shouting at me?"

That's not what I mean. My gut sinks when it feels like I'm the reason she wants to cry. I don't understand humans, but maybe I've upset her.

I shake my head. "No, that's not what I mean. Why are you upset?"

She sucks in a breath as if I'm asking something dumb. But...!

She says, "Maybe it's different for your species what was it again?"

"Kuqnil."

"Yeah... I suppose it's different for kuqnils. I know Earth isn't as amazing as your spaceship. But calling it backward isn't that nice. So is making me stay here with you when you didn't ask me first."

But it is easy to see that staying with me is better. I can protect her, and—

She stands. "Can I have some time to myself? I just want to be back on Earth and enjoy my vacation."

I shake my head, even though I would much rather make her happy. "No, you are here to stay. If you want a vacation, we can go to some planet for us to have the vacation together. I can't let other humans see me on Earth."

She stares at me with fiery intensity as if she is shooting a laser from her eyes. I don't understand. What's wrong with her?

She says, "You don't get to tell me what to do and you don't get to make it sound like you can determine what happens to me. I may agree to be here if you ask nicely. I don't know whether all kuqnils are like you, but you don't get to grab me and put me here, forcing me to be your mate."

What the hell is wrong with her? She should understand she is my mate. The mate bond should go both ways, and I can't be the only one feeling it.

I roll my eyes. "You know you are my mate. I don't understand why you are trying to fight it. You can feel the bond like I do."

She shakes her head. "That's what you think and what you like to assume. I hate it when beings try to pick my life for me. Maybe you are a strong male, you don't get to do that to me. Maybe I'm what you called your mate, but you still don't get to do that to me."

What's the big deal? This snobbish human female thinks that she is better than me?

I'm about to say something when my marks burn again, screaming for me to slow down instead of hurting her with my rage. "How do humans claim their mate?"

"Well, we don't have mates like you do, I think. Most of us aren't crazy enough to kidnap whoever they want and demand that they be their mates."

Is she calling me crazy? I—

She continues, "We ask if that's what each other wants. Imposing our wishes on others is rude. Even the males don't do that."

Oh... Maybe that's because those males are too weak and they don't care for their mate. When kuqnils find our mate, we claim them as ours and we protect them. There's no imposing our wish when the mate bond should have put us together already. She's just delusional and trying to resist me.

I suck in a breath. I'm a pretty amazing kuqnil. How can she act like I'm not good enough for her? I stand and she stumbles back, putting distance between us.

I head to her. She is soon backed up to the wall. I stop when I'm a few steps away from her. "Are you scared of me?"

She nods, and she is shaking. The cape on her makes it obvious. My mate should enjoy my presence, not be scared of me.

She says, "You are a lot bigger than me and it looks like you want to hurt me."

I shake my head. "No, that's not what I want to do. Like I said, I just want you to understand that you are my mate, and we are meant to stay together. I don't know why you are hesitant about that."

She sighs. "I guess you really don't understand. All you want is to lock me up and make me your mate, whatever that means to you. You don't care how I feel about that."

My mate seems to be incredibly stubborn and not very smart.

Hm... Maybe that's because she's a human.

I've met humans that are pretty smart though.

I rub my temple. "I don't understand what your problem is. But if you want some space for yourself, you can stay in my room."

She shakes her head. "I want to stay here on my own."

No, she should—

Maybe I should do the thing that she calls listening to her. "Fine, if that's what you want, you can stay here. I will come back later."

It hurts me to see her upset, but it also hurts when it looks like she doesn't want me.

I head to the door, pressing the button for it to open. I glance at her when I put a foot out of the door. She sits on the chair again, looking at the wall that's away from me, not even caring that I'm leaving.

How rude...

Chapter 9

Zoe

I let out a breath when Iechon is gone. I check the door after it slides closed just to make sure I'm alone.

That's some crazy stuff there. Does asking for permission not exist among kuqnils? He's so mad that I don't feel the same way as him and he has been trying to make me feel something for him.

I pull the cape and rest my head on my arms on the table. What is happening? Why am I here? I don't want to be his mate. He is such a manic male... nothing feels good about this.

It feels like he could lose control at any moment and destroy me.

I sniff as tears drop. I've tried so hard to hold back my tears when it seems like he will just be even more pissed.

I just want to get back to Earth, even though he despises my planet. But I'm locked here and there's no place for me to go.

I stare at the plate with what's left of the food. I don't think he cared enough to make me paella because I'm a human. He kidnapped me from the beach. Maybe he also bought food on his way out.

Well... Given how he acts like he's the king or something, maybe he just robbed the restaurant.

There is a warmth in my stomach. If that's the mate bond he mentioned, maybe I'm feeling it. It is different from how it felt when I dated before. But...

I don't want to be a mate to a crazy alien...

Maybe I shouldn't have let him fuck me. That probably let him think that I've signed up to let him do whatever to me.

I wanted that and I enjoyed sex with him. But it is different when he wants me to be his mate instead of just a hook-up. I thought... I thought this was simply a detour during my vacation, but...

I stare at the wall ahead, rubbing my eyes to clear my vision. Who can I trust and who will help me? I don't even know where I am. How do I get home?

Iechon

I take a deep breath when my heart is still hammering in my chest. It takes so much for me to leave her inside. When I caught her sneaking around in the corridor, she said she missed me. I thought that meant she knew what was happening.

Maybe she didn't.

Maybe she was flirting with me because she remembered that I had warned her to stay in my room.

Hmm...

"Captain."

I almost bump into Onner when I turn the corner. Why is he here again? Today, he has been annoying and has been following me around. I clear my throat. "What?"

"I was looking for you."

I scowl. "Is something wrong? The portal isn't showing up as predicted?"

He shakes his head. "That's fine. We are heading there now. I'm checking to see whether there is anything I can help you with."

I lift my brows. "Help me? About what?"

He looks down the corridor to where Zoe is. "Is everything fine? She doesn't seem to be doing well here."

I grunt. "Everything is fine. She is confused, but she won't stay confused for long."

"Captain, how much do you know about human females?"

"What's to know about them?"

He shrugs. "I bet you don't know a lot about them. You aren't a fan of getting to know other beings."

Yes, I don't care how others think about me, and I don't care about what they are up to. Onner is the one managing business relationships and I'm the one slashing through everything that dares to stand in our way.

Onner continues, "Humans are very different from us. So, if you want her to be happy and want to trigger the rest of the mate bond, you have to make her want to be your mate."

"I know that. I'm going to make her accept that."

Onner shakes his head again. "That's not what I mean. You can't just force that to happen."

I roll my eyes. "Really? Are you trying to mess with me? She's just in denial of our bond."

"Humans don't feel it the same way as us. You have to win her over. The mate bond acts differently to them. Most human couples don't even have a mate bond."

I grab his throat. "Do you think that you are an expert and you get to tell me how to treat my mate?"

He pokes my hand and doesn't seem to be scared of me. That's rude. But given he has been working with me for a long time, I'll give him that.

He says, "At least I know how to interact with other beings better than you. And I've asked whether you want to watch human movies with me, but you refused."

I groan and roll my eyes, letting go of him. "Yes, why would I want to watch those?"

He winks. "To prepare for a human mate."

I scoff. I never imagined my mate would be a human. "Get to the point. What should I do to win her over and make her accept that she's my mate?"

"Tsk, tsk." Onner shakes his head with a smug smile that annoys me. Now, he thinks that he has some trade secret that makes him better than me. He continues, "You can't think of it that way. You have to ask her."

"I did. I asked, and she was scared."

"You didn't ask; you demanded. It's different."

I still don't understand what the problem is. It must be those stupid human movies. "You've watched too many movies. Those are fiction and aren't real."

"Geez, that's not the point. Humans love those, so they have to be at least kind of real. In those movies, the male always does something for the female. Things that she will like."

I suck in a deep breath. What Onner said is useless. I've been doing that. "I take her as my mate. What else should I have done otherwise?"

He sighs as if I failed a test. "Something before you claim her as a mate. You have to show her that you care about her."

"That's why I claimed her as my mate! Come on!" I growl at his nonsense. If I didn't care about her, I wouldn't have taken her with me.

"No, not like that. You really should have watched a few of those movies with me. Before you ask whether she wants to be your mate, you should maybe offer a gift."

A gift?

Is that the same thing as how Zoe said I should have asked her first? And something about I shouldn't say that Earth is a backward place, even if that's the reality?

Onner continues, "And you have to let her know you care about what she thinks and what she wants. You can't assume that either. You have to ask her, nicely."

That's a ton of things I have to do when it doesn't have to be that complicated. This mating thing is stupid. "Anything else? Do I also beg for her to accept me now?"

Onner rolls his eyes. "Well, I'm not the one choosing for you to have a human mate. Try your best and get to know her as herself, not just the physical existence."

"Yeah, yeah, human expert." I scoff and continue my way down the corridor, back to the control room.

Maybe when Zoe said she wants to be alone, I should let her.

My cock twitches at the memory of how good she felt under me. She was happy, and she enjoyed our time together. Is she scared that I'm not a human? But...

I'm better than a human.

Well, I suppose she doesn't like that thought either.

Humans are so annoying.

Chapter 10

Zoe

I take a deep breath, holding onto the cape Iechon gave me. I'm alone and he hasn't barged his way back here. Maybe he is being patient with me.

Or... he's planning something else.

I have nothing with me. My phone and everything else were probably left on the beach when these green aliens kidnapped me. Iechon said it as if he is doing me a favor by capturing me.

My vacation and my life on Earth are pretty much over. I'm with a psycho alien who won't listen to me while wanting me to be his mate. Maybe all he wants is someone for him to fuck and show off to other aliens.

I sigh and squeeze my arm, which is sore after I rested on it. Am I a toy to him? Maybe this is worse than getting kidnapped by another human.

Well, I've never been kidnapped that way before, so it's hard to know which is better.

I pull the cape and wrap it closer around my body. I'm still in my bikini after all, and that's not the proper clothes here.

This room is cold, and the walls seem to be laughing at me. I can't flee from this place and I don't know who I can trust.

There is a knock at the door. I'm too tired to care and too tired to say a thing. If Iechon wants to come in, he'll just do that. I thought he knew I wanted to be on my own, but I guess not.

It quiets down for a bit before a rapid knocking comes again. "Are you fine inside there? Zoe? Fell asleep?" It is Iechon.

There is a nudge in my stomach. Part of me, strangely, wants him to be here and hold me in his arms. When I flirted with him, he wasn't that annoying. The hair behind my neck stands and shivers. Iechon isn't a human, and I didn't realize until... So...

Maybe that's the reason for the load on my chest. Something feels wrong.

"Zoe!" Iechon is shouting outside when he should be able to come inside.

I sigh. What's his plan now?

"Come on in."

The door slides open and he runs in with big strides. "Are you okay?"

He's so confusing.

I nod. "Yes, I'm fine. I thought you'd come in on your own."

He scratches his head. "Well, I figured I should ask first." He clicks his tongue but says nothing more. It doesn't sound like he wanted to ask me, but he did.

I lift an eyebrow at him. "I think I got nervous when I figured out you're actually an alien and not a human."

He lifts his hand as if he is going to say something that will involve his gestures, but he soon puts his hand to his side and sits on the chair at my side instead. "What's there to be nervous about?"

I stare at him. Everything? I thought he would be mad at me already, but he seems to be controlling himself.

He reaches for my hand, slowly, so slowly that it feels like he worries that he will break me. This is quite a difference from how he was before. What changed?

He finally takes my hand in his. "I'm sorry if I've scared you. I don't mean to. Maybe I should be smarter and know that you and I are very different. You are also different from other humans I've met before that are from other planets."

My heart picks up speed. Part of me is glad that he seems to be understanding, but part of me... It feels like he is trying for something. Is it that... he figured that he has to switch tactics to make me his mate?

There is warmth inside me when he is a lot gentler. It probably goes against his nature, but he is trying.

He wraps his arm around me and pulls me to him. "I think you have questions. Maybe you should ask those."

I frown. Maybe he is trying to be nice, but I'm not sure how long that will last.

He waits for a moment, but within seconds, he holds my hand and pecks a kiss on the back of it. "Don't worry. I'm not going to get mad and I'm going to be patient."

Well...

I snuggle up to him, resting my ear on his chest. I can feel the vibration of his heartbeat, and it warms me more than it should. I squeeze his thigh. "This is actually kuqnil flesh and not human with green paint all over it or something strange."

He sucks in a deep breath. I grimace. So much for saying he won't get mad. Maybe I shouldn't say that when I'm pretty confident that he isn't a human, but... Somehow, I feel the need to reconfirm that. When I used to hurry to save lives, I made sure to ask for clarification so everyone was on the same page.

He sighs. "Yes, maybe I have some features that look like a human, but I'm not a human." He leans close to my ear. "When you felt my cock in you, that was one hundred percent a kuqnil cock, nothing human-like."

My breath halts and a stream of heat burns my cheek. When I'm staring at his thigh, I can't miss how his cock twitches. I glance at him. There is a fire in his eyes, which also lights me up.

He isn't wrong. The ridges on his cock can't be fake, otherwise, when he pounds me... the fake parts would probably fall off.

I ask, "Why is your cock colder than the rest of your body?"

He scowls, and he stares at his cock. He is in his trousers, but he is definitely staring at that. "I have no idea. I'm born like that and I think all kuqnil cocks are like that."

I put my hand on the bulge. His cock is cold, but he is hard. "This isn't a costume."

He doesn't say a thing, but he lets me stroke his huge monster. "I don't understand why you think that I'm a fake kuqnil."

"Well... I've never met an alien before. I didn't even know you existed."

"Poor— I mean, I understand. It is okay to not know everything. I have never imagined that I would find a mate on Earth. Most of the time, we find a mate that's our own species, but it doesn't matter. I feel it inside me."

I don't know whether I feel it inside me. I liked being with him when we were flirting and when I still thought he was pretending to be an alien. "How does that feel? How do you know?"

He blinks. "I just know it. You should too. But you are human. Maybe that makes it different. It is okay if you don't feel that now."

Maybe? I don't know.

He strokes my side. "Do you have more questions for me?"

"What's the expectation for me? I'm the only human on your ship, right?"

He nods and my heart races even more. That doesn't sound too fun. "Don't worry about that. They will respect you. You are my mate, so you will stay with me. Otherwise, I don't have any expectations for you. Let me take care of you, protect you, and do things for you."

So... he's looking for a girlfriend? Looking to marry me?

Before I can blink, he presses a kiss on my lips. I almost melt from how hot his lips are. It feels right to be kissing him, and it feels like I should do something like this more. There is a faint vibration inside me that shouts at how good it will be if I let him take care of me.

But... that will mean I'm losing my freedom and this male is going to arrange everything in my life. I don't want that.

He pulls away and lifts his brows. "Is everything alright?"

I blink, only to realize that I'm sitting on his lap. Maybe I moved when we were kissing. His hard cock is right there, teasing my pussy. "I'm still trying to process everything. Since you take me here and I won't be back on my vacation, what I said still stands — you are here to keep me entertained."

He chuckles. "I can entertain you, and I'm glad you aren't scared of me. I think you are going to enjoy learning new things about beings and planets that exist outside of Earth."

I hope I'm doing the right thing. Iechon isn't a human. I'm supposed to be a mate to this alien. Everything...

I shudder when he squeezes my ass. He pecks another kiss on the tip of my nose and says, "I want you to know that I care about you and I want to get to know you more."

His words warm me. Or maybe it is how his cock twitches right under my body. His presence keeps doing strange things to me. I should probably stay mad at him for longer than this, when he was a screaming psycho a while ago. But...

He runs his fingers along my cheek. "Give me a chance? I think I forgot you aren't a kuqnil for a while."

"Would you treat a kuqnil female like that? Take her as your mate just like that?"

"She would understand and we would be working out things. But it's okay, everyone is different."

I rest a hand on his muscular chest. He is still the huge alien male that... burns my insides and wants to be mine. A bit too hard to imagine when I was back on the beach, trying to enjoy myself.

I say, "You would be planning everything for her and making her do what you want?"

He sucks in a breath. I shiver, waiting for him to scream at me. Maybe it has been long enough that he will forget what he said earlier. He lets out a sigh. "I'm not like that. I think it will be different. Maybe I'm just mad at how you keep saying I'm a human, and I don't like that."

"I don't mean to say that. I just..." I rub his chest and run my finger along his tattoos. "I can't believe that I'm an alien's mate."

He wraps his arms around me and pulls me to him. "Yes, you are. Onner said I should have watched some of those human movies with him. Maybe I should have, had I known."

I burst out laughing. "Human movies? Do you mean those... I hope he won't think every bit of those is accurate."

"Onner is a smart kuqnil. But maybe there is a point or two in those movies that are real."

I roll my eyes, but there is a warmth in me that grows. Maybe Iechon is really trying and we can work something out. "Just so you know. You don't get to make decisions for me."

He clicks his tongue with a naughty smirk. "Not even if I tell you to ride my cock like a sexy little human?"

Fuck him! "Just like that? That's all you can do to me? I thought a kuqnil captain would be capable of more."

He growls, and he picks me up, putting me on the table on my back. "So much for that. You were naughty and I'm going to punish you. Hope you aren't banking on me forgetting how you ignored my warning."

Fuck! I really thought I'd distracted him enough that he wouldn't remember. "I told you I missed you and I was trying to look for you."

He undoes the buckle that holds the cape together and pulls it off me, leaving me in my bikini again. "That's what you said, trying to flirt with me and to convince me to forget about that. I'm telling you that it isn't going to work on me and I'm still going to punish you and make you scream."

He leans close to my pussy, breathing hot air over me. The thin fabric of the bikini bottom does little to shield me from his teasing. I'm soaking from the hot breath and his scorching gaze only makes me burn hotter in lust.

"Tell me you want me." He chuckles as he keeps staring at my pussy. "I'm a patient kuqnil, so..."

I squirm, even though I probably shouldn't make it easy for him. But... "Fine, come entertain me with your cock."

"You love to keep control, huh?" He presses his thick thumb on my pussy, rubbing my wet entrance. "Look at this cute wet spot here between your legs."

"That's all you can do? Staring? Oh!" I moan when he pinches my clit.

"So naughty. Maybe my mate also loves to be punished and loves to be a brat." He yanks off my bikini. This table must be rigged. When he stands tall, his cock is right there in front of my pussy.

I spread my legs for him, reaching my own hand there and sliding my finger between my wet folds. "Are you going to do something? Or maybe all I get is to stare at you while I please myself."

He grabs my hands and pins them above my head. "No, you don't get to do that. This is my pussy."

His giant cock rubs my entrance. His cold cock sends electrical sparks down my spine. I used to think that a hot cock is what would fuck me a new one, but... Fuck!

He presses his tip into me, almost as if he is shoving a sword into me with how cold he is, but without the pain, only the inkling of pleasure and the promise of what he could do to me.

His huge cock stretches me as he goes deeper. I wrap my arms around him, arching to take him into me. The deepest part of me is hungry for him. His cock twitches and he grunts. Maybe he would also love to shove his full length into me, but...

"Zoe... You are so tight, so perfect. And, it feels like I may break you if I start doing what I want at this moment."

I gasp. My pussy squeezes his huge monster cock. "Do what you want to me. I'm not that fragile."

He grunts. "There are times I think I should take you seriously, but when it comes to this... You have no idea." He starts moving inside me, slowly picking up speed when I get wetter for him. "You are so perfect. Zoe..."

I like how my name rolls off his tongue. I hold him tightly to me. "At least you're kind of entertaining."

"Kind of. How insulting." He starts hammering in long, hard strokes. "You should learn to control your mouth."

"That's how I love to control my mouth, duh."

He grunts and picks up speed. "So naughty." He reaches for my throat. I move to let him hold me. "I love my brat."

"Mmm..." My body tenses when the ridges on his cock rub me harder and harder and pleasure swarms through me. "You have a fucking annoying cock."

"What?" He slams in a few hard thrusts. "It makes you scream a bit too much? This is your punishment."

I scream when he keeps hitting the deepest of me. He's driving me crazy with the pleasure and he definitely knows that. "Iechon!"

"You love me."

"Your cock, probably."

"How rude," he growls and pulls out of me right when I'm getting close to another orgasm.

I kick and squirm. His cock is right there, an inch away from my pussy. But he holds me down with his large hand, making me stare at him while getting nothing.

"Iechon! How dare you!"

He chuckles. "You know you need me."

I grit my teeth, resisting the urge to say something. I hate to let him have that much control over me. But... lust burns inside me and it makes it hard for me to think straight. How can his cock do something like that to me?

His green cock with the ridges that will please me is there, twitching, laughing at how I can't get that inside me.

He grunts. "You are such a tease."

There is a vibration inside me. It seems to come from deep inside my chest, something stronger than lust that pulls at me. I stare at him. His eyes darken even more than before, looking like he is going to chew me alive and I'm going to enjoy that a bit too much.

I gasp when my body seems to tense. It is different from how it feels when I'm enjoying his cock.

He leans closer. "Can you feel that? It's the bond."

Is that? Maybe?

"What does that mean?"

"You are mine and you want my cum."

Fuck! I hate how he's probably right. It's so annoying when it feels like I'm losing control. "Iechon… Fuck me."

He chuckles, his laughs are almost growls that shake me from the inside. "Yes, my mate. You will get everything you want."

He shoves his cock into me and makes me come almost at once. "There's no need to deny yourself pleasure."

My toes curl and my eyes roll back when there is another beep. I flinch. Iechon also stops pounding my pussy, and he turns to the door.

There is a shuffling noise, followed by a mechanical noise that sounds like it is from a machine. "We are getting ready to enter the portal. Please get ready."

Portal? What portal? The ones that will zap us into other places like those in movies?

What preparation? How do I get ready?

Iechon grunts. "How rude." His cock twitches inside me and he turns to me again. "You are on a table now. I suppose that's enough preparation."

Huh?

I'm about to ask when he starts hammering into me again. His huge cock pins me onto the table, making me take his strokes again and again.

"My mate only has to be prepared for me."

"Iechon! Argh!" I scream when orgasm takes over my senses. Everything seems to blur, leaving only the pleasure he keeps putting into me.

The table shudders under me, but I no longer know whether that's because of the portal or that's because of how hard Iechon is pounding me.

"Zoe... The portal won't stop me from taking you. Nothing will."

I shudder when he shoves his cock into the deepest part of me and his cock pulses with cum. "Iechon..."

Warmth spreads through me. Maybe this is how the mate bond works. The more time I spend with him, the more... it feels right.

It feels like I belong here, belong to him, and I get to enjoy him whenever I want.

Chapter 11

Zoe

When I open my eyes again, I'm not staring at the ceiling of the meeting room now.

My body is sore and my limbs are heavy. I move my arm, but...

I can't move that an inch.

What happened?

Did Iechon sell me off or chop off my limbs...?

Oh... I stare at the head next to me. Iechon is sleeping and half of his body rests over my arm and half of my body. No wonder I can't move my arm.

I let out a breath, letting his warmth and the warmth from the blanket sink in. I'm in his bed now. So... Maybe I passed out from the pleasure.

Hmm...

I close my eyes, trying to figure out what happened between the sex we had in the meeting room and here, in his bedroom.

I...

All I remember is how good his body felt, nothing else.

It must be his problem. His cock is the reason I don't remember a thing. I don't like that, but it isn't like I can resist him.

I stare at his face, which is mere inches away. He is a handsome alien. He wraps his arms around me as if I may disappear when he's sleeping. Something about that warms me.

He is such a huge male that he can wrap his body completely around me. It is comfortable to be here with him.

I want to stroke his hair, but it feels like I may wake him. he is the captain of this ship and he wants me. Am I the lucky one?

My brain hurts when there are that many things happening around me. I have to grab myself and make sure I understand and accept that other species exist and there are many of them out of Earth.

That's crazy.

I pinch my thigh and I wince from that. I'm not dreaming.

I suppose I should have figured that out, but...

Everything is so unreal.

How is this supposed to work?

Iechon is clothed and seems to need sleep. Is he that tired after he took me at the table?

I'm... not naked. I have the bikini top with me, but I'm in trousers. When did that happen? He dressed me up when I was out? That seems a bit creepy.

"Zoe..."

I blink when I finally look at him again, pulling my attention back to him. "Hi, you woke up."

He smiles. "I do. Maybe I should learn to control myself, but I can't. When you are around, it's a bit too hard."

I shrug. "It's okay. I hope I didn't wake you."

"Mm... You didn't. But you've been tired, right? And you said you liked these trousers."

Huh?

He squints at me. "What? I let you pick something and you said brown was better than gray."

"I don't remember picking. I don't even remember walking out of the meeting room."

He scowls and taps my forehead. "Are you fine? You were awake when I carried you out of the room. Do you still remember the portal? We left the room after the ship left the portal."

I shake my head and snuggle to his chest. He strokes my hair with worries in his eyes. I sigh. "Maybe I'm too tired. I don't remember anything after you came inside me."

"You don't even remember the bath?"

What bath?

He moves closer to me, looking into my eyes. "Are you sure you don't remember a thing?"

"I really don't remember anything."

"Well, are all humans like that?"

I roll my eyes. "I'm not always like that. Maybe it is you testing some drugs on me and knocking me out. Happy your plan worked?"

He huffs and rolls his eyes. "After I carried you here, I bathed you and cleaned you up before I put clothes on you and put you in my bed." He frowns and closes his eyes for a brief moment, so maybe he's also trying his best to remember what happened. "You fell asleep when I put you in bed. But I didn't figure that you wouldn't remember a single thing."

I shrug. I suppose that's not very important when I'm fine and I'm here with him. "I think it isn't that bad when I wake up to see your face."

"Oh..." He grins. "Really? I'm happy to hear that."

Ah... I think I can get used to this.

There is another beep from the broadcaster. This time, I don't jump and try to flee. Maybe these green aliens aren't here to hurt me after all.

"Everyone, we are getting ready to land. Please get ready." There is another beep, which signals the end of the broadcast.

Iechon sits up on the bed. "Are you ready? We're landing at a space station. Maybe we can get you some clothes."

Oh... Space station...

"Will there be a lot of other aliens?"

"You can say that. You should try to act normal."

"Okay." I think I can do that. For Iechon, acting normal probably means I shouldn't ask everyone whether they are humans in costumes.

"And..." He scratches his hair with a frown. "Don't tell anyone that you're from Earth."

I scowl. "Why? I know Earth isn't a place with advanced technology, but it isn't such a shame that I can't even mention it to anyone, right?"

He shakes his head and holds my hand as if he thinks I'm going to be mad and leave. "Not at all. You shouldn't tell others about Earth because... Well... um..."

I snort. Despite saying he is a patient kuqnil, he isn't one with patience. With his quick temper, why is he taking the time if he intends to be honest with me? "If I don't know and don't agree with the reason, I'm not going to do that. You don't get to make me do things without a good reason."

He watches me for another moment before he sighs. "There's a reason most humans on Earth don't know about our existence. We're supposed to leave them alone."

Hmm... So... Maybe it's against some rules for him to interact with me, let alone take me and put me in his spaceship and in his bed.

I lift my brows. "You aren't always a rule follower."

He swallows. "I'm a perfectly good kuqnil."

That's not an indication of whether he is a rule follower or not, which means he probably did break some rules to get me.

I shrug. "It's okay, I won't tell anyone."

"Good." He gives me a hand and helps me off the bed. "You're going to like it there. You can try new food too."

My stomach rumbles. Food sounds like a good idea.

I hold Iechon's hand tightly. His large hand comforts me. We're in a space station now. It looks like an indoor stadium with a tall ceiling. There are metal pillars going across the ceiling, keeping the structure in place.

I suck in a deep breath. The air is cool and dry, but perfectly fine to breathe.

Around me, there are aliens of all species and all colors. Most of them are larger than me. Iechon seems to fit better among the other aliens than I do. My heart hammers in my chest and my hand is sweating.

As we walk down the aisles, we go past stalls upon stalls selling strange things. The beings around me are talking in languages I don't understand. All of them combined. This is a loud place with a lot of different noises. I'm so tiny here that it isn't even funny.

There are occasional gazes on me. Maybe they don't always see humans walking among them.

Iechon squeezes my hand. "Are you fine?"

"Is the air better up there?"

He chuckles. "You look nervous. Don't worry. Most of them are nice beings and won't hurt you. Humans are smaller compared to other species, at least that's usually the case. That's not to say that there aren't smaller species."

I hold onto my cape. It feels a bit safer when I'm in trousers now. They're long for me, so I have to wrap the end in order to fit without the risk of falling. The cape covers most of my body, so I can only hope the gazes on me aren't due to my fashion taste, or the lack thereof.

Iechon is in his trousers and cape. Under the cape, he is wearing a strip of leather that goes diagonally across him, from shoulder to waist. It acts as another pocket for him, and he has a gun clipped onto that. Other than his trousers, he also has his belt, which holds yet another gun. There are a few more devices hanging on his belt, which may also be weapons.

It makes me nervous that he finds the need to bring all those with him. I've asked, but he said the space station is safe.

I take my eyes away from his belt. I should be looking at new things, not him. "I still think I may be dreaming, even though I know I'm not."

He smiles. "You're so cute. I like that about you."

"What are we doing here? Shopping?"

"Yes, I don't know whether there will be a store that sells clothes that will fit you better. And we can look for some with cartoon lizards."

I roll my eyes. "It doesn't matter if we find dinosaurs on them. I think they're cute, so I bought that bikini."

"Oh, I see. I don't understand why you like those. I thought it was some type of symbol, maybe good luck."

Given how dinosaurs are extinct, I'm not sure how lucky they are. "Not really. They're just interesting. And they're dinosaurs, so not exactly lizards. They don't exist on Earth now."

He blinks. "Oh, I see. I think I know dinosaurs. Onner sometimes talks about those human movies with dinosaurs."

"You've never watched one?"

He shakes his head. "No, I'm more interested in seeking business, not watching movies."

That doesn't sound very interesting, but maybe I can get him to watch something with me and we can sip beer together. He is the one saying that he wants to learn more about humans.

I stop at a stall which is hosted by a large boulder man. He is gray and his body is made up of large pieces of rock. He gives us a nod but says nothing.

On the table, there are a lot of baskets with rocks. They are cut into cubes with different minerals there.

Iechon squeezes my hand. "I don't think you want one."

Oh... "But these are interesting rocks."

"And tasty," says the large boulder shopkeeper. "Though... I don't think your species will enjoy them."

Um... Tasty...? "These are snacks for you?"

He nods. "Yes. Not many understand us, but we are special the way we are." He picks up a block with black rock and red crystal infused. "This is what I pride myself with. Sweet with a dash of spiciness. I've always wished to share the joy of it with other species, but that won't happen."

This is... interesting...

Iechon squeezes my hand again as he nods to the shopkeeper. "Thank you for introducing us to your food. I will be sure to let any of your kind know of your store when I run into them."

The huge boulder smiles and nods, putting the block back into the basket.

We walk away, dodging a few spiky beings. I say, "Do you get scared or worried when you run into species that you don't even know existed? It must be impossible to know every species."

"When I started traveling, sometimes, some of them were concerning, but once you get used to seeing different species, it gets better." He eyes me up and down. "But maybe if you were larger, you would feel safer around others. No worries. I will be here with you and no one will hurt you."

I nod. I don't doubt him when he holds me tightly and keeps me by his side. "Will there be other humans?"

He looks around. "I have no idea. There aren't a lot of humans around here. There are a few planets with more of them outside of Earth, but as a whole, humans are rare."

"Why? Are kuqnils rare?"

"I'm not sure about the reason. Kuqnils aren't that rare in this part of the galaxy."

I have no idea whether he is right, but there is another kuqnil on the other side of the aisle and it seems like Iechon doesn't know her.

Iechon points at a shop behind the stalls. "That looks like a clothing shop. Maybe we can get you something."

"Sure." I'm not a big fan of looking at clothes. Whatever lets me move around freely is good for me. But if he wants to get me something, I guess we can take a look.

It is a shop with bright lights. There are rows and rows of clothes. There are quite a few already here look around. There is soft and cheerful music in the background, but I don't recognize the instruments. Anyway, it's good music and I'm not picky.

I lift a hanger to check out the trousers. It feels like a pair of jeans, but it's lighter than it looks. I flip it to the back. There's a hole where my ass would go.

Iechon chuckles. "Looks like these are for beings with a tail."

Hmm... Looks like it.

I don't have a tail and I have no interest in showing off my panties for others to see. I put the hanger back on the rack and continue down the aisles. Iechon puts a hat or two on himself, staring at the mirror.

"You look pretty good with this one." I hand him one that's a lighter shade of green but shaped with horns to the side.

He tries it on. "You like horns?" There is a light frown on his face. If I say that I do, maybe he will try to grow horns just to please me. He probably won't, maybe I'm thinking too highly of myself, but...

I shake my head. "Horns are fine, but no horns are fine, too. It's easier to snuggle without horns."

"Right?" He grins and returns the hat to the rack. It is a tall rack, taller than me, with some hats I can't even reach.

I look up at the signs that are hanging from the ceiling. The shop is divided into sections with clothes that will fit different species according to their features. There are icons on the signs, making it easy to understand.

Some clothes are designed for someone with a tail, some for wings, and some... There's a huge rock symbol, so maybe those are for the large boulder beings. There are words on the signs, but I don't know the language.

I point at that and ask Iechon, "Do you know those words? I don't see them offering more options in terms of language."

He follows my fingers and nods. "It says, if you have any specifications, let the shopkeepers know. That's a pretty common language here, maybe within five galaxies."

"Oh..." Five galaxies sound like a lot, but from the way he talks about it...

He shrugs. "Five galaxies aren't that small when it comes to having a shared language, but that one has been promoted for years. Most traders know it. When it comes to traveling, five-galaxy isn't that bad. We use portals most of the time, so distance can feel different."

I nod, though I don't grasp everything.

We go to the section with clothes that will probably fit me.

We turn the corner to see a winged male sitting on a tall stool. His wings are like bat wings. It would be pretty cool if he could fly with those. He has a red T-shirt on with the logo of the shop. He gives us a nod.

Iechon points at me and says something. That winged male gets off the stool and pulls a measuring tape out of his pocket. He measures my height and points at the aisles behind him, saying something that's probably the instruction for which side to look at.

Iechon nods and we head to that side. After we are a few steps away, he says, "He says they don't have a large selection for your size, but maybe you can fit into the smaller sizes that are for larger species."

"I think it isn't easy to have a clothing shop when there are so many different needs."

"Agreed. But maybe this space station is busy enough for them to stock some of everything."

We arrive at the row of clothes and I scan through them. There is a beep from Iechon's phone. He scowls and pulls it out to check. He squeezes my shoulder. "I'll be back soon."

He picks up the call and hurries his way to the exit of the shop. Maybe it's something urgent. I can only hope it isn't something bad.

I stare at the racks of clothes again. It would be a lot more fun if I was back on the beach with my beer. I also miss my phone. If I tell my friends that I'm here with an alien, they'll probably laugh at me.

"Hey, miss."

I turn around to two large blue males. They are humanoid like me, but they are clearly not human. "Yes? Are you talking to me?" I think they are, otherwise, they will probably use some other language.

The two of them exchange a glance. "We've found some clothes that may suit you. Come with us."

I scowl and shake my head. "I'm fine. Thank you, but I'll start here."

One of them lifts an eyebrow. "We saw you with that green one. Are you in danger?"

Oh... Are they here trying to help?

Will they bring me back to Earth if I ask for help?

My heart races as blood rushes to my head. Iechon isn't around. If I'm looking to flee and get back to my life, maybe this is the only chance I will get.

But...

The two of them scowl. "Yes or no? It looks like you don't speak the language here, so... Did he capture you?"

I shake my head even when Iechon did take me from the beach. "Stop bothering me."

They make a move, but before I can run, one of them punches me in the gut while the other covers my mouth.

I kick at them, and one of them hisses in my ear. "Bitch, stop it."

An electric shock runs through me like the first time Iechon tried to capture me. Strength leaves me, even though I try my best to struggle. They are taller than me and a lot stronger.

Where is Iechon?

Chapter 12

Iechon

Stupid call.

I put my phone back into my pocket, letting out a breath. I wish I didn't have to take the call, but it was an important client and I can't risk losing the relationship with them.

I go back into the clothing shop. Maybe Zoe has already picked out something. I turn the corner next to the cashier. I think that's the quickest way to get to her.

This is a stupidly big store, and I hate that. I understand that shops try their best to make beings walk around and spend time looking at different things, but there's no reason to make stores into a maze.

I take another corner, and I think I'm where I left her. But...

Zoe isn't there.

My heart skips a beat when the marking on me starts burning. I take a deep breath and hurry to the nearby aisles.

There's no one there and not a hint of Zoe.

My ears twitch as I try to capture her sound, but the music in the store is too strong.

I run down a few more corridors, but she isn't in sight.

Blood runs cold inside me, and my mind draws blanks. She is gone... Maybe...

My head hurts. Maybe she was lying to me. Maybe she never wanted to stay here with me. She had to when there was no way for her to leave on the spaceship, but now that I gave her a chance...

Why did I leave her alone?

I let out a sigh as I meander my way to the exit of the shop again. If Zoe doesn't want to stay here and be my mate, maybe I should let her go.

There is a pulse of heat inside me, and it feels like my body might explode. Zoe is my mate and I won't find anyone else to replace her... Maybe Onner is right. I should have asked her instead. She hates how I make decisions for her and...

At a side door, there are two blue beings. They... seem to struggle to get out of the door. Why are they walking out of the door with their bodies stuck together?

Unless... they're holding something between them.

There's a scorching pain inside me that screams and shouts. A fury of rage brews inside me, even though there's no reason for that other than how Zoe left me.

I run to those creatures regardless. Something inside me shouts at how I can't leave them alone.

They see me, and they hurry out of the door. It doesn't seem like they are moving along just so I can get out of the door.

"What are you doing there?" I growl at them. Something fishy is happening.

One of them pulls a gun at me. I duck behind the wall of the shop so the laser hits the rack instead.

I sweep my leg at one of them, only to hear a scream. Zoe!

She is kicking, and she is the reason these beings were walking funny!

I pull out my laser gun and fire at these two blue beings, but one of them hoists Zoe in front of himself so I can't shoot at him.

These fucking males!

The other points his laser gun at me. "Drop your weapon before we kill her."

I clench my laser gun but have to lower it before they will hurt Zoe...

That one continues, "You are lucky we aren't reporting you. You know that humans are out of reach."

What?

Fuck... Are they from the Patrol? If they find out I kidnapped Zoe...

The male that's talking picks up speed and follows the other one as they drag Zoe with them. He snorts at me as if I'm dumb.

Zoe is struggling, but she is getting weaker by the second.

Am I... standing here and watching these two take her away from me?

Zoe is my mate...

No one gets to take her from me!

Fuck them Patrol team!

The moment those two turn around, I grab a stool by the wall and throw it at the blue male. He yelps but falls on the floor like a brick.

Before the one holding Zoe can do a thing, I fling the stool at him. He ducks with Zoe in her arms, but holding her slows him and I kick the laser gun off him.

I smack the stool at his head, so hard that my hands hurt.

Before Zoe will drop to the floor with the male, I yank her to me instead.

"What is happening here?"

There is a growl followed by rapid footsteps. I turn around with the stool in my hand. Well... the legs of the stool when I seemingly broke it smacking at the blue males.

There are a few from the Patrol here. They are of different species, but all with uniforms.

I suck in a deep breath. Are these here to help those two blue ones?

One of them nods and two come to Zoe and me. I hold her tightly to my side. "Those two tried to kidnap her."

Zoe is panting and leaning on me. She nods. Her mouth opens and closes, but nothing comes out of her. There is a weak spark from her. Maybe these two used a taser on her, so much so the remaining spark is still lingering inside her.

The Patrol looks at each other. Maybe these aren't here to help the two blue males. The one with a star on his jacket comes to me. "Leave her to us. We will get her checked."

I shake my head. "No. No one takes her away from me."

Zoe makes a weak noise, but she is too soft for us to hear her.

The leader leans down to her. "Miss, can you answer me?"

"He..." Zoe gasps and shivers.

This is when it hits me. She can tell the Patrol that I kidnapped her and... I will be in deep trouble and she will get to go back to Earth.

I close my eyes, hoping I won't look suspicious. I'm still holding her and she is a bit too weak to keep herself upright. I can't leave her and let her slide to the floor, either.

I know she is my mate, but what if she really doesn't want to stay with me? Maybe she thinks that my pointed ears are ugly, or she doesn't like how I don't have horns.

Maybe she still hates that I kidnapped her...

"Miss, are you alright?"

Another of the Patrol team comes with a chair. We help Zoe sit. The chair has a back for her to lean on, but she holds my hand and pulls me to her. She is shivering. Those blue males must have scared her.

The captain of the Patrol has a deep scowl on his face. "Miss..."

Zoe takes another breath while I hiss at the captain. He doesn't get to make Zoe talk if she's exhausted or frightened. If he tries something more—

Zoe squeezes my arm, gesturing for me to stay quiet. "Those two tried to kidnap me. I fought them, but..." She gasps again, as if she may die from lack of air.

My heart races with hers as if we are sharing the same heartbeat. It hurts me to see her in pain.

She rubs my side. "Iechon arrived just in time and saved me."

Oh...

The captain nods. "I see." He looks at me, then behind me. I follow his gaze to find the others from the Patrol have cuffed the two males. The captain says, "We will handle these two. We've been trying to locate them. They've been left alone for a bit too long."

I scowl at those two. They are still on the floor, not moving an inch. I would love to think that I've smacked them hard enough. But maybe the Patrol team used something on them to keep them down. "Traffickers?"

The captain sighs. "That's what we believe. I don't think these two are the ones behind everything either. But stay safe out there. I know humans are rare, but... Just be careful when you're walking around with her."

I nod. There have been beings like that. I know a few myself. Not that I like what they are doing, but... "I will make sure she is safe with me."

Zoe gives me a smile. Her eyes are almost closed, but that's from how tired she is. It must be scary to be captured by two blue males that are both larger than herself.

I hold her closer to me. "I'm sorry."

The captain clears his throat. "Not trying to interrupt, but we will take care of everything else. Have a nice day, and you can leave now."

I pick her up, holding her in my arms. She wraps her arms around me and gets comfortable.

Had I not left her alone, maybe nothing would have happened. I don't think those two would have made a move if I were there with her.

In my arms, her chest rises and falls. Maybe she has already fallen asleep.

I let out a breath. At least she is safe with me now. I look around in the shop. Most beings are around again. The two blue males who tried to kidnap her are gone. The stool that I broke remains on the floor as the only trace that something happened.

The winged male who I talked to earlier is here. He watches me and Zoe. "Sir, I... I hope everything's alright?"

That's not an easy answer. "Do you know what happened?"

He nods. "I saw you fighting them, but I was too nervous to help. I... I called the Patrol."

"Thank you." I glance at Zoe, her cute sleepy face melts me. I think my arms are pretty amazing, but maybe she would be better off sleeping in a bed instead. "I don't mean to create a mess here."

He shrugs. "A mess isn't a problem. Maybe you can get her something, as an apology. We should have done better."

Maybe. But this is a space station, so... some dangers and risks are expected. "I don't know. I was just looking to get her something new."

"Give me a moment." He flies through the aisles and is soon nowhere to be seen.

I guess as long as I get Zoe something that will fit her well, I've accomplished what I set out to do...

Chapter 13

Iechon

The walk back to the spaceship feels like an eternity. I growl at whoever dares to stand close to me as I make my way through the market again. I have Zoe in my arms and I can't afford to have anything happening to her.

If only I can keep staring at her face as I walk.

"Hey! Watch out!" Someone growls at me.

I hiss back at them. They should know better when I have Zoe in my arms and they should be able to see that I'm going to need more space.

They stare at me with their ugly and dumb tentacles as if they don't see how dumb they are. But as soon as they peek at Zoe, they turn around to leave.

I don't wish to get into a fight with anyone if that means Zoe may get hurt. But I really want to punch that dumb tentacle thing.

Maybe I should control myself. There's nothing more important than putting Zoe onto a bed and letting her rest. Poor thing... It doesn't help when my absence is a large part of how that even happened.

Had I not taken that call... she wouldn't be hurt.

I'm such a bad mate. Such a bad kuqnil that maybe I don't even deserve to be the captain of the spaceship.

Maybe I smashed at those two blue males, but I'm not sure whether I smashed them hard enough to avenge Zoe. I didn't check whether they were still alive. I'd rather they stay alive, so I can maybe smack them again the next time, even harder. Or maybe I caused them permanent damage, and I could hope for them to suffer longer.

I suck in a deep breath, forcing myself to slow down. My heartbeat is racing a bit too much and blood is spiking through my brain, so much that it almost hurts. I need neither of those.

The Patrol has gotten those two and I hope they will punish them further. Maybe I should check on their progress, but for all the time I've been a trader, I only relied on what I could do on my own. No one else is as reliable.

Not that I don't trust the Patrol to do the right thing. Well...

I'm not sure whether I trust them.

It will be annoying if I get into trouble with them. But there are limited things they can do to me. I'm a strong kuqnil, and my fleet is powerful, too.

I shrug as I give a nod to someone passing by, who gives a concerned look at Zoe.

"Captain!"

I turn around to see Onner waving at me. He wades through all the beings, almost stepping onto a tail or two before he arrives at my side. I give him a nod, even though I'd rather not talk to anyone.

He watches me and stares at Zoe. She is still resting in my arms, seemingly asleep. There is a faint bruise on her neck. It must be because of those two males.

A fire burns inside me again, even though there's nothing I can do about the situation at this moment.

"Captain, what happened? Is she tired? I don't suppose you had too much action with her out in the open."

I scoff. I'll always want her, but I'm not that crazy for sex that I would initiate when there are other beings around. "No, that's not the case. We should get back to the spaceship before we talk."

"Okay...?"

"You will make sure we get back there as soon as possible. Get these beings to move and pave a way for me."

"Fine, fine."

I stare at poor Zoe as she rests on our bed. I'm sitting on the bed by her side while Onner sits on a chair nearby. I told Onner everything that has happened. I think I spent a lot of time talking, but apparently, it's not enough for Zoe to wake up.

Maybe I should be a bit more patient. But I'm never a kuqnil of patience.

Is she fine?

Onner sighs. "I can't imagine that can happen to her. She must be frightened."

"I think she is. The taser must have tired her out. I hate for that to happen." I also hate to let anyone know about that. It doesn't make me look like a good kuqnil and I'm supposed to be a good role model for the rest of my fleet. Yet...

I continue, "Maybe I should have skipped picking up the call, or just picked up the call next to her."

Onner shrugs. "I don't blame you. If she isn't ready to join us, it will be safer for her to not know everything about our business."

I stroke Zoe's hand. Her skin is still warm and I can feel her pulse, but it doesn't make it easier when she is still down. There is a weak smile on her sleepy face. I will imagine she is doing as fine as possible.

Onner says, "The healer has checked on her and everything looks alright. You don't have to worry about that. Nothing is damaged."

Yes, I know that's the case, but I still worry about her and I doubt that feeling will fade anytime soon. I need her to be fine before I can think about other things. Even though I know she will wake up very soon, maybe in hours, my heart is still racing and my mind is blank half of the time.

Onner chuckles and I glare at him. There is nothing funny about this.

He clears his throat. "I think you probably understand what it means to be her mate now. From the movies you despise, this is what happens. You can't stop caring about them."

I fight myself to not punch him in the face. How dare he compare me to those fictional characters?

He doesn't seem to care, though. "But it's going to be fine."

I don't know how it will be fine when Zoe is still fighting to recover. If only I could make myself leave the bed, then I would teach him a lesson. He thinks that he is a friend when there are no other kuqnils around, and he's getting a bit too comfortable around me.

He peeks at Zoe again. "I think she will understand."

I don't know whether she will. "Are you sure?"

"Maybe you have to ask her to make sure. More importantly, are we keeping her on the ship?"

I hiss. "Yes, I've told you, she is mine and I'm keeping her."

"Have you asked her?"

I probably should. When she wasn't where I left her, I almost got a heart attack. I have to make sure she will stay here... Or... make sure I know whether she wants to stay here.

Onner clears his throat again. "Remember to ask. In those movies, the human female will tell you what they think."

I scowl. "Even though I'm a lot larger than her? And though she has no place to go when we are on the ship?"

"Well..." Onner scratches his ear. "I think that should be how that works. You should do something romantic, too."

I huff and roll my eyes. Zoe didn't find me going to Earth and picking her up as romantic, so... humans have different tastes and I have no clue what they like.

He chuckles and pats my shoulder. "Or just ask directly before you screw up more."

I grunt. All he said was a whole lot of nothing. "Go away and do your work."

Onner stands from the chair. "Sure, Captain. Are you going with me?"

I stare at Zoe and shake my head. I can't leave her alone even though we're on the spaceship already and have set off into the galaxy.

When will she wake up?

Chapter 14

Zoe

Ouch... My head hurts. It feels like I got run over by a truck and my whole body is screaming, so much so I can't even move.

The last thing I remember is Iechon showing up, then I kicked and tried to get to him, but then...

Hmm... I think I ended up in Iechon's arms.

After that...

I hate to always be the one getting smacked around by aliens that are a lot larger than me. If only I could be the one smacking those two.

Something hot touches my cheek. I shudder and force my eyes open. Everything is blurry. There is a huge green face right in front of me.

I almost jump, until I recognize Iechon. "You scared me."

"Oh... I'm sorry. I just wanted to make sure that you were doing fine." Iechon squeezes my hand with a deep frown.

"I think I'm doing fine. You are here with me, so I think I'm fine."

"Really?" His frown deepens, and he doesn't seem to be happy with my answer. "Are you sure? You said I scared you."

I shake my head. "It's just... I don't seem to remember what happened. It feels like that happened a lot recently. I'm supposed to be on vacation, but everything that happened is more tiring than when I was at work."

I push against the bed to sit up. My arms are sore, but I'm not hurting. Iechon wraps his arms around me, steadying me and helping me sit up when my muscles are all cramped. "What happened?"

"That's what I'm going to ask too. What happened? When I finished the call, I couldn't find you in the nearby aisles. So I searched further away. Found those two blue things walking funny. Then I figured they were trying to kidnap you. I fought them and saved you. The Patrol arrived and captured them."

I shiver when the memory swarms back. Iechon kisses me, holding me with his comforting arms.

"Don't leave me," I whisper.

The pull in my chest is here again. He holds me and rests his forehead on mine. "I won't. I thought you wanted to leave me. But I'm glad I didn't give up and leave the shop just like that. I'm so sorry."

I sniff as tears swell in my eyes. I could have ended up kidnapped by those beings and sold somewhere dangerous. My luck has been wonky recently, and I needed to fix that quickly.

Iechon sits on the bed and wraps my body in his. "I will make sure nothing like that happens again. I'm so sorry I didn't take good care of you. I should have been more aware of how dangerous it could be in the space station."

"That's why you brought two guns and probably some more weapons."

I think we're back on the spaceship now. After what happened, he probably won't want to stay there for long.

He sighs. "Yes, it's a strange place. No one really rules over there, so everyone fends for themselves. Usually, nothing will happen when everyone assumes everyone else is armed. But maybe you look harmless enough that they bet their luck on you."

He continues, "I'm such a bad mate and a bad kuqnil."

I squeeze his hand. "No, stop saying that. You aren't. You tried your best, and you didn't want that to happen either. I'm safe. All is fine."

"But..."

"No buts. You tried your best." My heart is still racing at the memory, but it would be wrong to blame Iechon.

"You should be mad at me."

"I'm not. Would you rather I be mad at you?"

He remains quiet. I bite my tongue to keep quiet as he thinks over whatever he finds important. I don't want him to feel bad about that, especially when he already saved me and I'm safe.

He sighs, his hot breath tickling me. "No, I don't want you to be mad at me or upset. But... maybe you are right. I've tried my best to fix the situation."

"And you've done amazing."

He pats my stomach, but he falls quiet again. I take the moment to gather my thoughts and enjoy his presence. Maybe being an alien's mate isn't that bad. There are dangers, but he will try his best to save me. If I'm with a man, I don't know whether he can smack two huge blue males to get me out of there alive.

I snuggle into him. "That was a scary place."

"You'll get used to that. Not getting attacked, but get used to fighting for yourself."

I let out a sigh. "I'm used to fighting for other people's lives, but when it comes to my own, I don't have a lot of experience."

"Really?"

"Yeah, before you grab me off the beach, I used to save lives as a paramedic."

"So, you are good at putting limbs back together?"

"Well..." I laugh. He is cute in some way. "Not like that, but rush them to the hospitals. And to try my best to keep them alive on the way."

I lean back on him, stroking his arms that are wrapped around me. "Now, I'm here."

"I..." Iechon's voice shivers. "I want to ask you some-thing."

"Sure." My heart skips a beat. Is he going to ask what I have in mind?

I close my eyes to see how he ran to save me again. This time, the memory is a lot clearer. I can even see how he smashed those two males with the stool. Not what I'd expect for beings fighting in space, but Iechon risked getting shot by laser guns to save me.

He holds me closer to him as if that's possible. He remains quiet, but there is a vibration in his chest that echoes in me. Is he nervous?

He pecks a kiss on my neck, but he is still quiet. I hold his arm, stroking him. He has been looking like a hulky, muscular beast that won't flinch at anything, but...

"Zoe..."

"Yes? Whoa!"

He spins me around so I can see his face. "I know we had a bumpy start. We didn't meet like humans and I'm not even a human. But I know in my blood that you are my mate. I understand that you may not want to be mine and..."

He sucks in a deep breath as if the words are weighing on him. "Zoe... Will you give us a chance? Be my mate?"

I look into his eyes, feeling the heat inside me. I have no idea what will happen next if I agree to be his mate, but if I refuse...

A pain nudges me when I give that some thought. Maybe I don't want to leave him, even though I don't understand everything there is to know about life in space.

"Iechon... I..."

He sucks in a breath as if he is bracing to get punched. "Yes? No? Do you need more time?"

I cup his cheek. He watches me, seemingly in doubt. "Iechon, I'm nervous too. But I can feel it inside me. I don't completely understand the mate bond, but I want to give us a try. Thank you for saving me, even though it was dangerous."

He wraps his arms around me so tightly that I feel like a teddy bear getting crushed. Maybe he should remember that I'm a human and I'm a lot smaller than him. I don't mind if he thinks I'm fragile in this instance.

"Thank you, Zoe. I promise it is going to be amazing. I run around on trading routes doing different jobs for merchants. I think you will enjoy it. We will get to travel around and you will be able to visit many interesting places."

That sounds like a good deal.

He kisses me before I can say another word. His lips are hotter than I remember, and he is melting my heart with the kiss. There are waves inside me that are stronger than the ones on the beach. His warmth envelopes me and I love that.

"Zoe, I will take good care of you. No one gets to take you away from me."

"Iechon... I know you will be there for me."

He pulls me over as he lies on the bed. "I'll always be there. No more stupid blue males."

I rub his cock, which has been pressing against my body as he held me close to him. "Look at this. You've never hidden your intention."

He grins. "I knew exactly what I wanted the moment I saw you. There's no hiding. I don't do that, I take what I want."

"As a proud and snobbish kuqnil?"

He rolls around and pins me under his huge body. "Soon, that will be a horny and strong kuqnil."

"Maybe also one that's obsessed with me."

"Are you complaining?" He pulls at my clothes and I move to make it easier for him. I love looking at his handsome face and... the warmth in me agrees.

"I'll complain when it gets boring. You're supposed to be here to keep me happy and having fun."

He grunts and grabs my boob, nibbling on my flesh. "If you enjoy screaming and squirming, you will be having fun. You are such a tease."

"Come and fuck me with this hard cock. Rub me with your ridges."

I try, but I can't reach his cock. It's too far away. I'm too short and my arms are also short. How frustrating.

He chuckles. "Maybe you are the impatient one."

"I'm just trying to make you feel better, horny kuqnil."

He growls and rubs his thick tip against my entrance. I'm so soaked that maybe I should be ashamed of myself. But I want him. Whether it's the mate bond or not, I know what I want.

"Zoe, if you keep being such a tease, you will regret it."

"That's what you've kept saying. Nothing is going to change unless—! Yes!"

I shudder as he shoves his cock into me. His ridges rub my walls and he feels amazing inside me. He stretches me in ways I can't even imagine and gives me all his pleasure.

"You just love to be a brat."

"You just love a brat!" I throw my arms around him, arching and moving to take him deeper into me.

I need his giant cock. He's the reason I started to love getting pinned on the bed by someone much larger than me. He can pound my pussy until I can't even breathe.

The ridges!

"Iechon! Fuck me harder!"

"Happy to do so." His cock twitches inside me and grows even larger. "I've told you since the beginning that you are going to love this."

"I will if you keep at it and get—! Oh!" I scream when an orgasm takes over. Maybe I should be mindful of the other kuqnils on the spaceship; it will be embarrassing if they hear my moans and screams.

Iechon's cock hammers into the deepest of me, pumping in the pleasure, making my orgasm last, and it's so good that I could die happy from it.

Fuck other kuqnils. If they are that unlucky to walk by, that's their problem, not mine. I'm just going to enjoy Iechon's amazing cock and the flame he can light in me that no other can.

"Iechon! Yes! More!"

"Oh, there's nothing I like more than that. Scream for me."

I do as he says. Not that I'd love to stroke his ego, but his strong alien cock is so good at making me come.

I grab onto his back and my nails dig into him when my body tenses to take in another orgasm. He doesn't flinch but only pounds my pussy harder and harder.

"My mate, mine!" He growls when something seems to shift inside me, clicking and sending dizziness through my head. Is something wrong? Am I going crazy?

He growls again, "Can you see that?"

See what?

I open my eyes to see him glowing in green. His tattoo glows and... I gasp. "You look like a Christmas decoration now."

He huffs. "I don't care about that. I'm not a decoration." His cock twitches and he slams in a few hard, long strokes, as if proving me wrong. "You are mine."

"Yes, glowing kuqnil, I'm yours. And bad news to you, you are also mine."

He chuckles. "That's not bad news. Say hello to your sore pussy."

"Well, that depends. Mm...!"

Maybe I should learn to stop teasing him, but I'm loving this. The more I rile him up, the harder he will fuck me. I don't understand how my body can take his size, but as long as it's working, I'm not going to look too deep into that.

"Iechon, your markings are glowing."

"I know," he grunts and takes a deep breath. "It's burning me and I need you to quench the lust inside me."

"Is that working?" My body shakes from how hard he's going at me. I think the bed is shaking, too.

"Maybe. I will know when I— I'm filling you up with my cum."

"Yes! Mark me as yours!"

Fuck... I'd never imagined myself saying stuff like that, but with him, it feels like the right thing to say. He can make me his fucktoy all he wants, and I'm going to enjoy that a bit too much.

His cock twitches, and his hot cum fills me up. My pussy squeezes around him, milking every drop for myself.

I gasp with my eyes closed, soaking in every bit of pleasure. "Iechon... Do I also glow?"

"I don't know. But I think you look perfect under me."

I smack his back. That's such a stupid answer. "Come on, you can see it. Am I glowing?"

"No, you aren't glowing green. But your body is so hot that it feels like you are melting my cock."

Fuck yeah!

"I love you."

"Same. That's the only thing you've said that pleases me."

"You just have an ego so big that my moans and screams don't even satisfy you."

"Your tight pussy will satisfy me. And you shall be punished with my cock all the time with what you've done."

"And what have I done to a huge kuqnil like you? Are you still pissed that I left your room when you warned me against that?"

He kisses me and my inside flutters from that. He is so good with me and I love his hot lips. "I'm not pissed, but I'm going to remember that and make sure I punish you enough."

"What's enough?"

"I will let you know when enough happens." He smirks, and I doubt that moment will ever arrive. Not that I care. I suppose he can fuck me for other reasons, or just for fucking sake. But...

"Iechon, you're the best."

"I know I am." He pulls out of me, watching my pussy with a wide grin. "Look at you, so perfect. I wonder whether you are the only one with a cute and tight pussy. Maybe this is a thing from human females."

He kisses my pussy, which is still dripping with his cum. "You are mine now. And we know that, finally, together."

I let out a breath, slowly catching up when the orgasm fades from me. Finally, I can use my brain and come up with more organized thoughts. "Maybe that's the reason you glowed. You need more than sex to glow, otherwise, you would have when we first fucked."

He tilts his head to the side and muses. "Probably. Maybe it took both of us to recognize that. You are my missing piece."

I wink and hold his hand. "Good. Makes me sound important."

He holds me in his comforting arms again. "Good. You are important to me. You are my mate, the one and only one in the whole universe."

I snuggle up to him. "The feeling is mutual. My one and only mate."

Epilogue

Zoe

The sea ahead calms me. The waves build and kiss the shore, making music in the air. The seawater spreads along the sandy beach before it slides back to the sea.

I wriggle my toes, feeling the silky fine sand. There is a cool breeze joining in the gentle crashing sound of the waves.

The water is a lot greener than those on Earth and the sky isn't as blue. But this is a beach regardless.

The star of this planet shines almost the same way as the sun does for Earth. Iechon told me the name, but I didn't remember it. Who cares what it's called, anyway? It feels like the sun and acts like that, so the sun it shall be.

I take a sip of my beer, letting the cool and slightly bitter liquid run down my throat. I lift my sunglasses for a moment to watch the sea. With the rise and fall of the waves, I think I can spend the whole day here.

"Zoe..."

I turn around to Iechon. He is also sitting on a beach chair, just like me. He is half-naked without the cape. It is too hot to be in one of those. With his sculpted muscles, he makes for a great view too, which makes it hard to decide whether watching him or the sea is better.

"Yes?"

He lifts a can of beer from the cooler. "Why do humans like these?"

"Kuqnils don't drink anything with alcohol?"

He stares at the can. "This is different. There are so many bubbles."

I snort a laugh, almost dropping my can. "You're crazy. Learn to enjoy life."

He takes another sip. "Sure."

I let out a breath and reach for his hand. He holds mine with his huge hand. There is no better time than spending my day here with him, my mate.

There's a fire simmering inside me. That happens all the time when he's around. I can feel his presence better than I can feel anyone else's. I think it has to do with the mate bond. For now, he is confused, but still in a good mood.

He puts down the can and gives my hand a squeeze. "What are we doing today?"

Huh? "What do you mean?"

He frowns at the sea and lifts his sunglasses to watch it. "Are we going to spend the whole day here, staring at the water?"

"That's called a vacation."

There are shouts. We turn, only to see a few kids of all species chasing a red inflatable ball. Maybe it's not too different from Earth after all. Kids are still kids.

I smile, watching a kid tackle another. One of them has horns. I don't even know what species they are. I only know that they aren't human, and also aren't kuqnils.

"Zoe..."

I turn to Iechon again. "What were we talking about?"

He sighs. "What's the plan for today?"

"Well, sit around and enjoy life."

"Staring at the sea and sipping bubbly drinks all day."

I stroke his arm and laugh. "I suppose that's another way to describe that."

"This is what you were doing before I sent my kuqnils to get you on my spaceship."

I nod. "Yes, and this is what I meant when I told you to repay me with the vacation I was trying to enjoy."

"I thought it would be fun."

"I think this is pretty fun."

If we were on Earth, he couldn't be here with me. He can't be walking around as a green alien. He would scare the kids and we would get into trouble. Worse trouble than if he got caught kidnapping me from the beach.

He scowls. "Maybe I shouldn't have told you there was a beach here."

"How selfish. What else should we be doing? I think we should celebrate our success."

He grins. "I think so, too. We can always celebrate." He lifts his can, so I toast with him. We both take a sip of the beer. He still frowns, but I think he will learn to appreciate a good beer soon. We went back to Earth to get those, after all, so they're the original ones.

"Iechon, I have no idea you ran a business like that. A security business?"

He shakes his head while I frown. We just helped a group of traders through an area that was said to be filled with space pirates. So...

He says, "I do whatever my clients want me to do and pay me to do. As long as I can make myself do those. So I don't have a fixed structure and no fixed line of work."

Ah...

"I see."

His gaze travels from my face to my t-shirt. I suppose I should wear a bikini, but... He pokes at my stomach. "I like this t-shirt."

I glance at the cartoon dinosaur with a wide smile. "I like it too. Still don't think it was designed with my species in mind."

"Well, it fits you well."

It does. I hold the edge of it and lift part of it. His eyes are glued to my bare stomach at once. I roll my eyes. "Come on, I'm just trying to get a better look at it."

He groans when I put the edge down. "You have had it for so long that I'm sure you know how it looks."

"It's the first thing you gifted me."

He takes a sip of his beer. There is a faint red on his cheek. For his green skin, it means he is blushing hard.

I narrow my eyes on him. "It's okay. I know you didn't buy it."

He clears his throat. "I didn't buy it, but I earned it in a way."

I roll closer to him. The armrest of the beach chair doesn't make it easy for me to hug him, but I try my best. "Thank you. I will treasure this t-shirt."

"I know you like cartoon dino... dino... lizards."

He is so cute at times.

"This t-shirt will remind me how you smashed two blue aliens to save me."

He squeezes out a smile. I hope he still remembers how it isn't his fault and I'm grateful to be here with him. I squeeze his thigh. "We'll spend the day here, just enjoying the sun and the sea."

"Sit here and do nothing."

"Are you here to spoil my mood?"

He grunts and murmurs something under his breath.

I wink. "And maybe after that, we will have something fun for you."

He glares at me. "You enjoy being a little brat."

I scowl in a dramatic way. "Mind your language, filthy kuqnil. There are kids around us."

He rests his thumb on my throat. "That doesn't seem to bother you when you were in that bikini with that much boob showing."

"You're crazy."

His touch lights a fire inside me again. How annoying when I'm trying to enjoy my day on a nice beach.

He lifts my chin with a finger and turns my face to him. "My mate, you know you want me now. We don't have to wait until the day is over."

"But the tourism advertisement said the sunset is going to be perfect, and I don't want to miss that."

He growls, "There are hours before sunset."

"You have no patience."

He leans closer and pecks a kiss on my forehead. "Yes, are you new here?"

"Stop ruining my day."

"Maybe some action is what you need to spice up the day." He stands and comes to me, probably planning to grab me and make us go back to the spaceship for whatever spice he wants to add.

I rub his cock, which is already so hard that it probably hurts. "No, we are staying here and you will love it a lot more after sunset."

I pat his seat. "Now sit back down, sip a beer, and chill."

He murmurs something more before he sits. "I should know you and Onner were planning something when you kept making me watch those human movies."

"It's working."

He sighs and sips his beer. I glance at his couch. The poor shorts are trying their best to hide his erection. When the sunset is over... It's going to be interesting.

Iechon

"Stop it! Stop!" Zoe groans and kicks in my arms. But we are on my spaceship now and no one is going to help her.

I grin as I make the strides to my room. I think some dummy designed the ship and must have put my room too far down the corridor.

"Zoe, my cutest mate, the sunset is over. Time to follow through with your promise."

She moans and punches me when we get into our room. I put her down on the bed and hover over her. She is a small human, but something about her never stops fascinating me.

She rolls her eyes and throws her arms to the side. "Fine, but you're just a huge alien bully."

My cock twitches. She knows what to say to make it tempting for me to devour her. Even though I know she is playing to my desire, I can't stop myself from getting hooked. "You love your alien bully."

She rubs my cock with her foot as if she isn't tempting enough. "What will the hulky alien bully do to a tiny human like me?"

I flip her over and pull off her t-shirt. I should have kept her naked, if only we weren't outside for that long.

"Hey! You be careful of me!" She purrs, and it makes me even harder. I don't even know whether she is asking me to slow down or urging me to go even harder with her.

"Don't worry. I will keep the t-shirt intact. But when it comes to you..." I nibble on the back of her soft neck. "Hard to say what will happen to you. I'm the evil alien bully, after all."

She moans when I shove my hand between her legs. Even through her shorts, I can feel how soaking wet she is. I yank off those annoying pieces of cloth. She is already dripping, so ready for me.

I free my cock, rubbing my tip against her entrance. "Look at you, can't wait to take my bully cock."

"Oh, bully me, come on, Iechon!"

I shove my cock into her. I used to worry that I would hurt her or break her, but her slutty pussy proves otherwise. I tried to slow down for her, but all she did was moan and squirm to take me in.

Her tight pussy sucks my cock and pulls me into her. Her walls are so juicy that she is massaging my length and my ridges. She likes it when I rub her with the ridges.

"Iechon! Yes!"

I tighten my grip on her neck. "So much for saying that I'm the bully." I pull from her until only my tip is inside her. "You want me."

"Yes!" she screams when I push all the way into her, slamming into the deepest part of her.

"Your tight pussy is so perfect for me."

"Oh, yes!"

I start moving inside her. I can take her even deeper and harder when I thrust from behind. She squirms and moves, but all she does is please me even more.

I grunt when a wave of pleasure sweeps through. "I've been so patient with you that it hurts."

"Oh!" She clenches the sheets when she can't reach me. I love that. When she struggles with the pleasure I pump into her, it is perfect. Maybe I shouldn't admit to loving her struggle, but when I'm the reason for that...

"You are sucking me with that tight pussy."

"Bad bully alien!"

I pick up speed, enjoying her slick folds. The more she moans, the harder I take her. She squeezes me when she comes on my cock. The markings on my body burn again.

After she agreed to be my mate, I could feel part of her mood and feelings. So... I shudder when it feels like even more pleasure piles onto me. So much more than our sex before we activated our mate bond.

"I love you, Zoe."

"Mm..." she murmurs something I don't understand. But I'm going to pretend she is saying the same.

"I'm going to fill up this tight pussy."

"Yes!"

Now, this is a lot easier to understand than her moans.

My cock twitches and I let go of myself. I can almost feel pleasure exploding inside her, so much so it also riles me up.

This is going to be our lives together now. On my spaceship, traveling to many different planets, I get to have her moaning and screaming my name.

I whisper in her ear after I emptied my load in her, "Maybe I like a good sunset and a nice beach."

She gasps and pants, her pussy squeezing me again. "I told you."

Maybe she's right.

Get a bonus story!

https://icepawpress.com/alina-riley

He doesn't even know what's an Easter Bunny but he hates my event before I can even host it...

This grumpy and annoying grey alien with a tail hates me the moment I show up at the doorstep of the community center. For him, any celebration is stupid. Except I'm going to host the party for the kids and I'm going to do it amazingly well. He won't get to stand in my way. Everything is going great until... my partner for the event falls sick... Now, I need someone to help me with the bunny costume...

Also By Alina Riley

A Mate For The Luraella Traders
Saved by The Alien Boss
Guarded by The Alien Boss
Rescued by The Alien Boss
The Alien Boss's Hook Up
Crashing into an Alien Tribe
Trapped by Snow
Caught by Fire
Stranded by Vine
Mated to the Baekex Bandit
Taken by The Alien Bandit
Saved by the Alien Bandit
Healing the Alien Bandit
Mated to the Zalcor Rebels
The Space Outlaw's Treasure

Also From Ice Paw Press

Dark and Steamy Paranormal Romance
The Wolf's Captive: Collateral

Urban Fantasy
The Hidden Order of Magic: Shaken
The Magic Rebel

Steamy Sci-Fi Romance
A Mate For The Luraella Traders
Crashing into an Alien Tribe
Mated to the Baekex Bandit

Dark Mafia Romance
Kneel to the Jarockis